EXTRA!

EXTRA!

by

GEORGE MORSE

Author of
Circus Dan

WILDSIDE PRESS

CONTENTS

EXTRA!

Chapter I

BIG NEWS

Don Durian, young managing editor of the *Porter Press,* looked at the clock on the opposite wall of the news room. In another half hour, at exactly three o'clock, the city final would roll onto the waiting presses in the basement two floors below.

Don glanced anxiously about the editorial office. From his desk, on a slightly raised platform at one end, he could see everyone and everything in the office. In front and to his right was the circular desk behind which Steve Garwood, the city editor, was wading through an increasing pile of local copy. To the left was the telegraph desk where a gray-haired editor bent over the long sheets of copy which the electric telegraph instruments brought into the office. Beyond these desks were those of the reporters, the sports editor, the society department and the various special editors which are required for a paper with a circulation of 130,000 papers every day.

The whole staff was working at top speed to make the deadline for the city final but despite this Don felt restless, anxious. There was something in the air that disturbed him. Perhaps it was the bitter campaign the *Press* had been waging to oust Marcus Krieg, owner of the opposition newspaper, the *Midwest News,* from his position as mayor of the city. Or perhaps it was the anxiety he had felt all week over the unexplained absence of his uncle, Robert Durian, owner and editor of the *Press.*

It was Thursday and Don's uncle had left the office hurriedly Monday morning. He had refused to tell Don his destination but had promised to be back in not more than three days. That morning a telegram, signed by his uncle, had come from Beldon, a city in the western section of the state, saying that he would arrive at 4 o'clock on the afternoon air express.

Don glanced at the clock again. Twenty-five minutes until the city final. Anything could happen in that length of time, an earthquake could shake half of the world, a king could be assassinated, a fast train wrecked, a mine explosion, an air tragedy. He paused at the last thought. His uncle was in the air then, speeding east toward Porter on the afternoon cross-state air express. Don forced the thought of any accident from his mind and turned to the urgent task of getting the city final to press.

A telephone on his desk shrilled. It was Ed Mc-Guire, police and city hall reporter, so excited he flung his words into the phone in a jumble, but Don, used to Ed's excitable ways, got the message. He reached for a sheet of copypaper and his pencil scrawled notes rapidly. This was big news! Have to make over the banner on the front page. He looked at the clock. Twenty minutes left. He must call the composing room to let them know a lot of extra copy was coming.

"What's that?" he shouted at the police reporter.

"Five killed and eight injured! I thought you said one. All right, keep on talking."

Steve Garwood, the city editor, had heard Don's exclamation and slid out from behind his desk to lean over the managing editor's shoulder.

The story was big. Five men killed and eight injured by an explosion in the light and gas plant. McGuire was giving them all the details. In less than five minutes he was through and Don turned to his city editor.

"Can you read my notes?" he asked.

Steve nodded.

"Get someone to type it quick," instructed the managing editor, "and then let the composing room know a big change is coming through for the city final. I'll write the new banner and the main head and a short editorial for the front page. We'll roast the mayor right. He owns the majority stock in the gas and light company and McGuire says it was plain carelessness and pinch-penny methods that caused the explosion. Not a safety device in the plant. Get going."

The city editor seized the handful of penciled notes and ran for his own desk. A reporter ambled into the room and Steve called to him.

"Wake up!" he yelled at Harm Nichols, the star reporter of the *Press*. "An explosion in the gas and light plant just killed five men. Don's taken the bulletins from McGuire. Here they are. Get busy and put some color into the story. I've got to have it in five minutes."

The cloak of lethargy which had shrouded Nichols' entire being was stripped away by the words. He became another man, alive and alert to the hour. He was under the spell of the deadline period and, fired with the enthusiasm of a big story, grabbed the notes and hastened to his desk. He scanned them quickly and then rolled a sheet of copypaper into his typewriter. He was a two-finger artist on the keyboard and he beat the machine unmercifully as he wove his story into one of those graphic, readable accounts for which he was famous.

Ed McGuire, Harm Nicholas, Steve Garwood and Don had worked together gathering evidence to break the mayor's hold on the city, a grip which was so strong they almost despaired of their task at times. Controlling the gas and light company and most of the members of the council, the mayor had built up a political machine which had ruled the city for a decade. The only man brave enough to defy him was Robert Durian of the *Press* and the little band of loyal young newspaper men he had gathered around him. They had hammered away at the mayor at every opportunity and that large and gross piece of humanity had become exceedingly angry at times. He had threatened the *Press* with libel and ordered merchants not to advertise in it but in spite of all his efforts, the *Press* had grown. Readers knew it as a fearless paper and an honest friend of the people and they told others about it. The fight between the *Press* and Mayor Krieg and his *Midwest News* had been watched by everyone in the eastern half of the state. Time and again the *Press* had appeared to have the mayor in a corner but each time he had slipped out and everyone was watching for some big coup by one paper or the other.

The office was in a turmoil. The last minute telegraph news hissed through the pneumatic tube to the composing room on the floor above. Don wrote new headlines for the front page, wondering all the while what the *News* would say about the explosion. The headlines finished, he wrote a short and bitter editorial, condemning the mayor, as head of the gas and light company, for failure to have safety devices in the plant.

Ten minutes to go! Harm Nicholas had written half a column in five minutes and the last of his copy was on the way to the Linotypes where it would be turned into shining hot slugs, then into the front page and away to the stereotyping room, the last stop before going on to the big press.

Don felt the tension easing a little. They would make the deadline with time to spare. It should be a smashing blow against the power of the mayor. The young managing editor's deep regret was that human lives had been lost and tragedy brought into the lives of at least five families. He steeled himself against the thought. A newspaper man must not have nerves or the scores of human tragedies which occur every day would wear him down in a month, a week, perhaps a day.

The city final rolled into the press room on time and the tension in the editorial office eased as it always did when the big edition for the day was put away.

Two of the electric telegraph machines ceased their chatter while the remaining one moved spasmodically as the market reports and late sports news came over the wire.

The city final, despite its name, was not the last edition of the *Press*. It was the big edition, the one read in all of the homes of the city, but the green sheet, which followed at five o'clock, carried the closing market reports and baseball scores. If anything unusual happened they made over the front page of the city final for the green sheet. As a rule the telegraph editor did all of the work for the five o'clock edition while Don devoted himself to writing editorials and in conferring with the city editor on plans for the following day.

But this day was far from average. There was the big story at the gas plant and more detailed stories and pictures would be needed for the green sheet. Don turned his attention to the task of directing the staff. Two photographers who had been rushed to the scene hurried in and outlined the pictures they had snapped.

"Have the engraving department give me a half page layout for the green sheet," he ordered as he picked up the phone and called the composing room.

"We'll have a complete front page make-over for the green sheet," he told the foreman, white-haired Tom Johnson, who was used to such emergencies.

"Any pictures?" asked Johnson.

"Half a page," replied Don.

"Have the engraving room hurry them up," urged the foreman. "They're getting mighty slow up there."

Don promised to see what he could do and phoned the engraving room to get the layout made up with all possible speed.

Steve Garwood hurried up.

"I'll have eight or ten columns of stuff on the explosion for the green sheet," he said.

"Cut it, cut it," snapped Don. "I've just ordered a half page layout of pictures for the four center columns. Edit your stories and run them around."

"I can't cut them," protested Steve. "They're all good stuff. Here, look at them!" He pushed a handful of copy toward the managing editor.

"Haven't time," replied Don. "I want to get the green sheet well along before I go to the airport."

"Uncle coming in on the afternoon plane?" asked Steve.

"Wired me from Beldon he'd be in this afternoon," said Don.

"He'll sure go after the mayor when he learns about the explosion at the gas plant," said Steve. "Personally, I'd hate to be in the mayor's shoes."

"I've felt that way about it half a dozen times," said Don, "but each time the mayor seems to wriggle out. Maybe he won't be as lucky this time. Is Ed coming in to write his story?"

"He just phoned that he was too busy. We've been taking his notes and writing them here in the office."

Don nodded and turned to a batch of proof that had been laid on his desk while the city editor returned to the buzzing telephones.

The presses in the basement came to life with a roar as they spewed the city final out by the thousands. The circulation department had been busy and in less than a minute newsboys were running down the street, crying the story of the explosion. A boy hurried up from the press room with an armful of damp papers, so fresh they were heavy and smeary with ink. He tossed two on Don's desk, several on the city editor's table and then went on through the room distributing them at the various desks where eager reporters seized them and turned to read stories they had written.

A great, black headline across the top of the front page told the story of the explosion. The story underneath was short but clear and concise, written with a power only Harm Nichols knew.

Don checked every page in the paper for mistakes, found two headlines switched on the sports page, marked them and sent the paper down to the composing room. As soon as the first part of the run was over the presses would be stopped and a correction made.

The foreman of the composing room hastened down from the floor above and made his way to the city editor's desk.

"You're swamping us with copy," he protested. "We'll never be able to handle all of it for the green sheet with the markets and late sports."

"We've got to get it in," insisted Steve, running his long, slender fingers through his curly hair. "I've been cutting and cutting and if I do any more I'll have every reporter on the staff on my neck. They're writing great stories about the explosion. Have a heart, Tom, give me a break."

Don heard the discussion and left his desk.

The foreman appealed to the managing editor.

"We'll never make it," he said, "if you keep on running out copy."

"How much have you ready now?" Don asked Steve.

"About eight columns," replied the city editor. "Everyone is on the explosion and the copy is rolling in."

"How much can you handle and still make the green final?" The managing editor shot the question at the foreman.

"About six or seven columns if you hold down the markets and the sports," was the reply.

Don stepped across to the telegraph desk.

Jud Brown, a veteran of twenty years on the desk, was sifting out the market reports. Don leaned down and shouted for Jud was extremely hard of hearing.

"Cut your markets and sports," he cried. "We're running heavy on local news for the green final. Big explosion."

Jud looked up and nodded. Nothing to get excited about. He'd been through too many big stories. They were all alike to him.

Don returned to the city desk.

"You'll have to stay in seven columns," he told Steve, "and that's final. Four columns for the front page and the rest on the market page."

"That's giving us a break," grinned Steve. "They'll eat up the explosion stories."

"And a lot of subscribers will eat me when they find some of their favorite markets aren't in the paper," said Don.

He returned to his desk and called the municipal airport. The cross-state express was an hour late and wouldn't be in until nearly five o'clock. That meant Don could stay in the office until the last copy for the green sheet went to the composing room.

The spell of the deadline gripped the office again. Copy flowed smoothly toward the composing room where the waiting linotypes transformed it into type. Harm Nichols, writing the main front page story from the notes Ed McGuire had telephoned, finished his copy and handed the last sheet to Steve.

"Great story," grinned Steve as his flying pencil made several corrections.

"Sure," smiled Harm, "if you don't change it too much."

"Your spelling," replied Steve, "has never been any-thing to brag about."

"And that," retorted Harm, "is why we have city editors."

At four-thirty the last copy for the green sheet went to the composing room and the entire staff relaxed. It would be a smashing front page with the pictures and the graphic stories of the disaster at the gas plant—a page that should make a sizeable dent in Mayor Krieg's power in the city for the *Press* took special pains to point out that the mayor was the principal owner of the plant.

With the green sheet out of the way, Steve went over to the managing editor's desk, where together they would plan for the next day, decide on assign-ments and special features and which reporters were best fitted for the various tasks.

Don was bent over his desk, writing rapidly in long-hand the editorial which he intended to use on the front page the next day. He was calling for a show-down on the tragedy at the gas plant, a complete in-vestigation with blame fixed on the proper parties and urging that state officials take a hand to insure the honesty of the investigation. The managing editor was tall and angular and his shoulders hunched together as he bent to his task.

Steve sat down on the desk.

"Better straighten up those shoulders," he warned, "or the first thing you know they'll have you in some side show as a freak."

Don smiled and straightened up.

"It is a bad habit," he confessed, "and I don't need to do it for my eyes are perfectly good. Get too in-terested, I guess."

Steve looked at his managing editor. Don was six feet one with brown hair and blue eyes that had the faculty of becoming a steely gray when his anger was aroused. There wasn't a bit of excess fat on his body and he kept in good physical condition by taking long walks through the city at night.

Some members of the staff were inclined to believe that Don had secured his position through influence with his uncle but Steve, Harm Nichols and Ed Mc-Guire, who really knew the young managing editor, were quick to change that view.

Don was a born newspaper man with a keen judge of news values and a splendid sense of fair play. He had started on the *Press* as a cub reporter when he finished high school and rapidly worked his way up until he was placed behind the big desk as managing editor in charge of the news and editorial policies of the paper.

Steve had joined the staff with Don and they had gone up together, working and fighting for every promotion, helping each other in every way possible and finding mutual satisfaction in whatever success they obtained.

Harm Nichols and Ed McGuire had come to the *Press* two years after Don and Steve but they all had one thing in common—a nose for news and the four had soon formed a friendship that was growing famous in newspaper circles in the middle west.

Don was tall and slender; Steve was short and thin; Harm was stocky and built like a prize fighter while Ed was a chunky little Irishman with just a touch of brogue and a thatch of blazing red hair. After a year together on the *Press* they had joined forces and rented a large apartment on the edge of the business district and it was from this that most of the plans and attacks which caused the unscrupulous mayor so much trouble were originated.

"What shall we do with the explosion story tomorrow?" asked Steve.

Don sat back in his chair and clasped his hands behind his head.

"There were eight injured," he said reflectively. "Keep a close check on their condition and I have a hunch that as soon as Uncle Bob gets back he'll get in touch with the state labor department and arrange for an investigation."

Steve whistled.

"That," he agreed, "would certainly make a front page story."

"By the way," he added, "you'd better start for the airport if you want to meet your uncle when the express comes in."

"Four forty-five," exclaimed Don. "I'll get under way right now."

He turned to the steel locker back of his desk and grabbed his hat.

"Have Harm and Ed wait until I get back," he told Steve. "We may have to do some work tonight."

Steve nodded and picked up a telephone which had been ringing insistently.

Don was half way across the office when Steve's cry stopped him.

"Don," cried the city editor, "a plane's just crashed in the Indian hills west of Akron. It may be the air express your uncle is aboard!"

Chapter II

WRECK OF THE AIR EXPRESS

The city editor's cry stopped Don short. What was that? An airplane accident and the green sheet was already on its way to the press room. Too late to pull it back and make over. They'd have to get out an extra. That meant another deadline to make that day.

Then the full significance of Steve's words struck the managing editor. The accident was in the Indian hills country, that rugged, desolate strip of bad land that slashed its way half way across the middle of the state. The route of the air express crossed the heart of the Hills. There was a chance of it being the plane his uncle was aboard! Don felt his throat grow dry and his brain reeled at the thought.

Without a word he turned and ran to his desk. His eyes raced down the telephone card which contained all of the numbers he called the most. He stopped at one. It read "Municipal Airport, Walnut 4545."

Don called the number and added, "Rush it, please."

Ten seconds later the manager was on the wire.

"Hello Tony," said Don, "this is the managing editor of the *Press*. We've just got a tip that a plane has crashed in the Indian hills country. Have you heard anything about it?"

Steve leaned over the managing editor's shoulder.

"The call came from our correspondent at Akron, just at the edge of the Indian hills," he told Don.

"Don't stall around, Tony," snapped Don when the airport manager tried to evade the question about the accident. "Was it the afternoon air express?"

The reply was a long time in coming and Don hung over the receiver, his feeling of alarm increasing momentarily.

When the airport manager finally answered, his voice was so low the wires barely caught it.

"We've just had a call from Akron, too," he said. "Farmer out there reported a plane crashed somewhere near him. It circled once or twice, then went up above the clouds, which were pretty thick, and the next thing he heard it crash. When it circled over his place he saw the numbers. They were NC1035 and correspond with those of our express which is due in about fifteen minutes. Of course there's a possibility of some mistake."

Don grasped the telephone so hard his fingers whitened and everything blurred before his eyes. Of course, there might be a mistake but in his heart he was convinced that the plane which had crashed in the Indian hills was the express on which his uncle had been hastening back to Porter.

The *Press* and its staff were embroiled in the bitterest fight of their career. What would they do if anything serious had happened to the publisher? The question ran through Don's mind again and again.

The presses in the basement came to life as they rolled the green sheet out by the thousands and the inborn newspaper instinct in Don asserted itself. He forced his personal feelings into the background.

Here was news even though it struck at home, involving his uncle in an accident so serious that he hardly dared to think of its consequences. The public must be told. The presses must roll again.

The airport manager was still on the other end of the wire.

"Tony," cried Don, "my uncle was on the afternoon plane. I'm coming out to the field in a few minutes but let me know if you hear anything definite."

"I know he was," replied the airport manager, "and that's why I hesitated so long about telling you. I'm still hoping against hope that it isn't our plane. I'll let you know of any further news."

Don hung up the receiver, his lips set in a tight line, his eyes hard, cool and gray. He was the perfect news machine again. Orders flew from his lips as though he was a field general directing a new attack against some unseen enemy. His foe was time. They'd stop the green sheet as soon as enough papers to fill the orders to the outlying newstands had been printed, make over the front page, put in a short story about the plane crash, than slap a big "EXTRA" head over the story and send the paper to press once more. If they worked fast it would be out in time for the newsboys to catch the crowds hurrying home from the stores and offices.

"How much did you get from our correspondent?" Don asked his city editor.

"Enough for a good bulletin," replied Steve in a voice that was none too steady for he sensed the strain Don was laboring under. "Some farmer in the hills heard the plane. The weather's thick over there this afternoon and the plane appeared to be circling. As a rule they speed across that country and that's what attracted the farmer's attention. Next thing he heard was a terrible roaring noise of the motor and a sort of shrieking sound. A few seconds later there was a crash in the timber."

"How far from Akron was it?"

"The farmer is about 20 miles out of Akron and in the heart of the hills. The plane must have smacked up some distance from his place, say a mile, maybe. Lucky for us he had a phone and the good sense to get word to Akron so they can send out medical help."

"Write half a column," said Don. "Tony Marlas, the airport manager, said they had the same report. The plane circled the farm fairly low then went up in the clouds and crashed a few minutes later. The farmer got the numbers when it circled over him and they correspond with those of the afternoon plane. Of course," added Don with a desperate hope that he hardly felt, "there is just a chance Uncle Bob wasn't in the ship. He might have changed his plans at the last minute."

"It's too bad, Don," said Steve, "but your uncle was aboard. We check the airport every afternoon for the list of incoming passengers to see if any notables are aboard. Your uncle was on when the plane left Beldon."

"Yes, I suppose so," Don said dully.

"I'm sorry," said Steve. "We're doing everything we can to learn details. I ordered our correspondent at Akron to start in a car at once and phone us as soon as he learned anything definite."

"Everything's set for the extra," said Don. "Get your story out as soon as possible and then let the paper go. I'm going to take Harm Nichols and go to the airport. They may get some word there before we do."

Don found Harm in the washroom and the star reporter looked up as he entered.

"Just cleaning off the grime of another day's toil," he grinned. Then, sensing from Don's expression that something very much out of the ordinary had happened, he looked anxiously at the managing editor.

"What's the matter, Don? You're white as a ghost."

"The afternoon air express crashed in the Indian hills," replied Don. "First reports indicate a bad smashup and I'm sure that Uncle Bob was aboard."

Harm dropped his towel in the washbowl where it floated unheeded.

"Why, that isn't possible," he exclaimed. "Your uncle is coming back today."

"That's just it," said Don. "It is possible. He was hurrying back by plane. I want you to come out to the airport with me. We've stopped the green sheet and Steve is writing the story and putting it out as an extra."

Harm slipped into his coat and followed the managing editor out of the washroom. They ran down the back stairway to the garage at the rear of the *Press* building where cars used by members of the news and advertising staff were kept.

A boy hurried down the stairs after them.

"Here's a copy of the *Midwest News*," he told Don. "Mr. Garwood said you'd want to see it."

Don thanked the boy and turned to Harm.

"You drive," he said. "I want to see what the *News* said about the explosion."

The reporter sent the roadster they had taken shooting through the jam of late afternoon traffic, nosing here and there between cars until he reached Roosevelt road, an arterial highway which went past the airport.

Don scanned the front page of the *News*. They had held their city edition until almost five o'clock. He could imagine what had taken place in the office of the opposition paper, for the mayor owned the majority stock in the *News* as well as in the gas and light plant.

The story in the *News* placed the blame for the accident on one of the men who had lost his life. It was unfair and unscrupulous and Don could see that the mayor had probably stood over the reporter who had written the story and dictated it word for word. The editors and reporters on the *News* were afraid to call their names their own for the mayor had a disturbing habit of walking into the editorial office and firing half of the staff without warning. If the mayor could be forced out of office and compelled to sell his business properties, Don knew that the welfare of the city would be served and he was determined to do it if humanly possible.

Harm swung the roadster off the main highway and they rolled through the broad drive and up to the administration building at the airport.

A clock over the doorway on the building pointed to five o'clock. The afternoon express was due but Don knew that it would never come in. The plane, crushed and lifeless, was somewhere in the Indian hills.

Tony Marlas, the chubby little manager of the field, hurried from his office.

"No further word about the plane," he told Don, "but we've just had another call through to Akron. It's storming hard there and the wires into the hills have all gone down. It will be hours before we know what's really happened."

"How far is it to Akron?" asked Don.

"About 70 miles," replied Tony, "and another twenty or twenty-one miles into the hills."

"Let's get back to town," Don told Harm. "We're going into the hills as soon as we can get there."

"I'm leaving in a car for Akron in a few minutes," volunteered the airport manager, "and there'll be plenty of room for you. Glad to have you go."

"Thanks, Tony," said Don, "but you won't move fast enough for us."

Harm swung the roadster through the airport gates and out onto the main highway leading back into the city.

"We'd better stop at the apartment and get into some heavier clothing," said Don, "for we're going into a rough country and with the storm it's going to be a bad night."

Harm nodded his agreement as he guided the speeding machine through the traffic. He turned onto a side street where he could make better time and in less than ten minutes they stopped in front of the apartment building where they made their home.

Their apartment on the fourth floor included a large living room, sleeping porch with four individual beds, two dressing rooms, a kitchenette and dining alcove and a bathroom. It was furnished in a manner which would appeal to any young newspaper man. The chairs in the living room were large and the fact that they carried the scars of many a good-natured rough and tumble battle did not detract from their comfort. A long library table fairly staggered under the load of books and magazines but the whole tone of the apartment was one of comfort. The management of the building furnished maid service and the rooms were kept as clean as possible when there are four energetic young men rushing in and out at all hours of the night and day.

Don and Harm got into heavy trousers and waterproof high top leather boots.

"How about our slickers?" asked Harm.

"I'm putting on an old sweater and then my slicker," replied the managing editor. "These September nights have the habit of getting pretty raw, especially in the Indian hills."

"O. K.," said Harm. "I'll be ready in another minute."

When they returned to the car they were dressed for

a night in the approaching storm, which even then was sweeping its way eastward out of the rugged hills. The sun was smothered in banks of rolling clouds and the wind was rising rapidly.

"Drop me at the front entrance of the *Press* building," said Don, "and I'll run in and see Harvey Hendricks and get some extra money for this trip. Then take the roadster around to the garage and get a coupe."

When they reached the *Press* building Don hurried into the business office. Harvey Hendricks, business manager of the paper, was still in his office.

"I'm sorry to hear about your uncle," he told Don as the managing editor entered.

"We're still hoping there may be some mistake," replied Don. "Uncle Bob's name was the only one on the passenger list when the plane left Beldon and so far there's been no definite word from the scene of the accident. Storm struck the hills right after it happened and all the phone wires went down. Harm Nichols and I are leaving at once and we'll need some expense money."

"Of course," agreed Hendricks. "How much will you want?"

"Fifty dollars ought to be enough."

"I'll get it right away," said the business manager. He stepped into the main office and returned a minute later with five crisp new $10 bills.

"Let me know by phone the moment you learn definitely what happened," he told Don. "I'll wait here at the office for news. I wish you had more time for there's something I'd like to talk over with you."

"I'm mighty anxious to start for the hills," said Don.

"I know you are," said Hendricks. "This will have to wait. Good luck."

Don hurried up to the editorial office. The presses were rolling again, this time carrying the extra which told of the wreck of the afternoon air express. A boy ran in with a bundle of papers and Don took the one which was thrust toward him. He didn't want to read the story. No use. He knew what it said and he could be sure that Steve had done a good job in getting out the extra. Wonder if the *Midwest News* had the story? He hoped not but there was no time to wait and see if they came out with an extra.

Steve was hunched over his desk, writing assignments for the next day into the reporters' assignment book. He looked up as Don approached.

"Anything new?" he asked. Don shook his head.

"Not another word at the airport," he replied, "and Harm and I are leaving at once for Akron. What's the name of our correspondent there?"

"He's Charlie Miller, editor of the *Akron Weekly Argus,* and a mighty good correspondent; probably the best we've got."

"And he's already on his way to the scene of the accident?"

"Right," said Steve. "If anyone can get in there and get the story, Charlie Miller is the man. Those hills are full of moonshiners and an outside newspaper man might get shot for poking around there at night or any other time, for that matter, but Charlie's been at Akron for a long time and everyone knows him. He's about 50 and looks pretty much like a human barrel; short and fat."

"Guess I'll recognize him then when we meet," said Don. "You take charge of the office while I'm away and have Ed write a story for tomorrow on the explosion. Give him all the leeway he needs and strike at the mayor as hard as possible. Get in touch with our state senator and see if you can't get an investigation by the state labor department. Don't overlook a thing. This may be our chance to force him out of office."

"We'll put dynamite in it," grinned Steve. "Be sure and get word back to us as soon as you can."

"I will," promised Don. "Harvey Hendricks is pretty much worked up about it and he wants to know the first word. He'll be down in his office so don't forget to let him know."

Harm had a fast coupe waiting at the curb when Don reached the street. There was the grating of gears, the slither of tires slipping on the pavement and they streaked away through the gathering dusk. Street lights had been turned on and the city was shrouded with the silence which sometimes precedes a storm.

The reporter behind the wheel sent the car skirting around the business district and then onto a state highway that led to Akron, a long ribbon of concrete that stretched twenty miles without a turn.

Once clear of the city, Harm tramped on the accelerator and the powerful coupe leaped ahead. Their headlights cut a swath through the gloom and Harm leaned forward slighty as the speed increased. Fifty, sixty, and then sixty-five; the miles vanished as they sped through the ominous silence.

Don kept alert for some sign of the breaking of the storm. It came with a roar that sounded above the noise of the car. He heard it before Harm, who had every faculty concentrated on handling the car.

"Slow up!" cried Don. "The storm's starting. Wind and rain. We won't have a chance if we skid at this speed."

Harm nodded and took his foot off the accelerator. The heavy vibrations of the motor ceased and the car slid through the night as though some mysterious, powerful force were behind it.

The night awoke to a bedlam of noise. The rushing of the wind increased until it screamed like a thing alive and in agony. On the heels of the roaring wind came the rain—great, blinding gusts that shook the car and almost swept them off the highway.

"Good thing you heard it coming," shouted Harm, "or we'd have taken the ditch if we'd been running fast when it hit us."

"We're only fifteen miles out of Porter," said Don as he looked at the speedometer. "If the rain keeps up it will take us three hours to reach Akron at this rate."

They bored steadily through the storm, which at times was so heavy Harm had to almost stop the car. He was thankful there were few cars out on the highway for it was impossible to see more than fifty feet.

The road started to dip and turn, which increased the difficulties of driving. At the end of the first thirty miles, Harm stopped and Don moved over behind the wheel. They resumed their journey and there was little talk. The wind was still of gale force and Don found it hard to keep the coupe from veering across the highway. No wonder Harm was tired after thirty miles of driving. Fighting the storm was no easy task.

When they were fifty miles out of Porter, they reached Middlefield, a village of some 500 people. Here lights gleamed through the wall of rain and Don swung the car off the main highway and stopped under the canopy of a combination filling station and restaurant.

It was five minutes after eight. They had made fifty miles in a little more than two hours. Cramped from sitting hunched over in the seat and peering ahead in the storm, they welcomed the opportunity to stretch their legs.

"Check the gas, oil and water," Don told the attendant, "and put in whatever is needed. We're going inside for a lunch."

They ordered hot beef sandwiches and milk, which was set before them several minutes later. The food and relaxation refreshed them and they prepared to resume their journey.

The man who had taken care of the car came in.

"You fellows are the only ones who have been through since the storm started," he said. "Where are you headin'?"

"We've got to get to Akron," replied Harm.

"You've tackled a real job," was the reply. "Whenever we get a good storm, the Coon river goes on a rampage and overflows everything in its valley and I'd call this quite some storm."

"No argument about the storm," grinned Harm, "but we'll take our chances with the Coon. How far is it?"

"About nine miles and if you get across that valley you won't have any more trouble getting to Akron. If the water's all over the road, which is most likely, you'd better take it easy. One of you walk ahead and

test the road with a stick. Course it's all paved but
I've seen the time when the old Coon's taken out whole
slabs of that road and moved it a couple of blocks."

"That would be inconvenient tonight," chuckled
Harm. "Got a stick I can borrow?"

"Borrow?" snorted the gas station man. "No, I
haven't but I'll give you one."

"Same thing," replied Harm.

Don paid the bill for their lunch and the supplies
for the car and they resumed their journey. The lash-
ing fury of the storm was over and it had settled into
a steady downpour that might last half the night.

Harm was behind the wheel again and as they moved
slowly ahead Don had plenty of time to think of the
airplane crash. He shuddered at the thought that his
uncle might be helpless under the plane at the mercy of
the storm with its terrific wind and relentless rain.
But surely someone must have reached it long ago. A
doctor would have started from Akron as soon as word
came and then there was Charlie Miller, the correspondent in whom Steve placed such great faith. Those
thoughts gave Don some encouragement as he wondered what had taken his uncle on the sudden and mysterious trip. And why had he gone to Beldon, clear
over on the western edge of the state? As far as Don
knew his uncle had neither business relations nor personal friends there. Could it have been in connection

with the paper's campaign against Marcus Krieg? Was it possible that his uncle had been after new evidence against the mayor? Just then Harm spoke.

"We're getting down into the Coon river valley," he said, "and the water's starting over the road now. You keep on the lookout on your side."

Don lowered the window and leaned out of the car. There was four or five inches of water running over the highway and Harm had slowed the coupe down to walking pace. Barley, which had been sown along the shoulders of the highway to stop erosion of the grade, marked the edge of the pavement.

The water was deepening and after several hundred feet of slowly moving ahead, Harm stopped the car.

"I'm going to get out and walk," he said. "You follow me."

"I'll do it," said Don. "The stick's on my side." He opened the door and stepped down onto the pavement. About eight inches of water was running over the highway and he was thankful for the water-proof boots he was wearing. Stick in hand, he walked ahead of the car, testing every foot of the way to make sure the safety of the road. Above the swish of the rain he could hear the roar of the angry river. They couldn't be far from the main channel and five more minutes brought the main bridge into the rays of their headlights. Don signalled for Harm to stop and walked back to the car.

"Water's getting higher every minute," he said. "There's no use for both of us to risk it going across the bridge. I'll take the car and you can walk back to Middlefield or stop at some farm along the way."

"Walk nothing," exclaimed Harm. "I ride and in this car."

There was no changing of Harm's mind by persuasion or plea and Don finally gave it up and walked ahead of the coupe again, feeling his way through the swirling waters which poured over the road.

The grade rose slightly as they approached the bridge and the water over the road lessened. The bridge itself stood well above the flood and when they reached the main span, Harm stopped the car.

"I'll take the stick and do the exploring from now on," he said. "You've been tramping through this stuff long enough; it's my turn."

Don was wet and cold and he welcomed the warmth and shelter of the enclosed car. Harm strode on ahead to test the west approach of the bridge and Don followed slowly in the car.

They could feel the bridge tremble as some large piece of driftwood, the trunk of a big tree or perhaps a portion of some farm building, was crashed against the piers by the flood in its fury. The current appeared stronger on the west side and Don hoped that it had not undermined the approach. They might be trapped on the bridge.

Harm had reached the west end of the bridge. Water was flowing over it in a torrent and he explored carefully with his stick. From the care Harm was using, Don sensed that something was wrong. He left the car and ran toward his star reporter.

"What's the matter?" he asked.

"Plenty," growled Harm. "As far as I can discover, the current has undermined a little of the concrete approach just at this end of the bridge and there's a gap of about four feet; just enough to let our wheels fall through and strand us here."

Using the stick to demonstrate, Harm showed Don where a slab of paving, about four feet long and the width of the entire road, had disappeared.

"The current sweeps against this end of the bridge with terrific force," explained Harm, "and the state's going to be lucky if this bridge stands up through the flood."

"There's only one thing to do," decided Don, "and that's to make a run for it."

"What!" exclaimed Harm.

"I'm going to back the car up to the far end of the bridge, get it going as fast as I can and hope that it will have enough momentum to jump across that gap."

"You're crazy," protested Harm.

"We'll be a whole lot crazier if we stay on this bridge much longer," replied Don as the structure trembled.

"Look here," he went on, "the grade drops rather sharply off the west end. If we have enough speed we can shoot off the bridge, jump this gap and land on paving that's still sound. It will make some splash and we may break the springs on the car. What do you say?"

"It's no worse than staying here and getting marooned," agreed Harm. "Let's go."

Don and Harm got in the car and Don backed it across the bridge. They would have a three hundred foot run and Don tested the motor carefully. Then he snapped off the dash light.

"Ready?" he asked Harm.

"Go ahead," came the reply from the figure hunched in the seat beside him.

Don stepped on the accelerator, shifted from low to second and the coupe gained speed rapidly. They roared across the bridge, the steel girders flicking past them at a dizzying speed. The car was guaranteed to do fifty miles an hour in second and Don gave it every opportunity to live up to its guarantee.

"Hang on!" cried Don as the headlights showed a black void beyond the end of the bridge.

The next second was an eternity of suspense. The water was just in front of the car, a swirling torrent of destruction. The machine left the bridge at better than forty-five miles an hour, seemed to hang suspended in mid-air for a moment, and then crashed into the water.

Sheets of muddy colored water flew in every direction, spurted up through the floor boards and cascaded through the partially open windshield, but the car was on firm ground. The danger at the bridge was past.

Don disengaged the clutch and they coasted through the water which covered the highway.

"Swing left, quick!" shouted Harm, who was leaning out the window.

Don jerked the wheel over.

"Now straighten out," directed Harm, who dropped back on the seat.

"Better stop," he added. "That last one was too close. I thought we were going off the grade."

They rested for several minutes and then Harm took the stick, got out, and walked ahead to explore the road. This continued for the next half hour until Don heard a shout from his companion. When the car reached Harm he looked ahead and saw the highway free of water.

Harm climbed into the coupe and they left the valley of the Coon, with its menacing flood, behind. From then on until they saw the lights of Akron they made good time and it was just nine-thirty when they rolled into the village and stopped at the first gasoline station on main street.

An astonished attendant came out and gapped at the mud-covered car.

"Where in the dickens did you fellows come from?" he asked.

"Porter," replied Don. "We're a couple of newspaper men up to find out what we can about the airplane accident in the hills this afternoon."

"You mean to tell me you came all the way from Porter in this cloudburst?" said the startled villager. "How'd you ever get across the Coon river valley?"

"We almost had to swim," laughed Harm, "but we got here. What about the plane accident?"

"I can't tell you much about it," replied the attendant. "Heard a plane crashed in the hills about 20 miles west of here near Phil Hunt's farm. He phoned in about it and said he was going out and see if anything was left of it. Then the storm struck and all the phone lines in that part of the country went down at the first puff of wind."

"How can we get to Hunt's place tonight?" asked Don.

"You can't," was the reply. "There isn't a car made that could get over those hill roads. It's bad enough in good weather and just plain impossible now."

"But we've got to get there," said Don. "My uncle was on that plane."

"Well, now, that's too bad," said the sympathetic

villager. "Charlie Miller, the editor, and Doc Hanson started out as soon as they got word but got stuck a mile out of town. They came back and got horses and started again."

"Then where can we hire horses?" asked Don.

"You'll never be able to get in there alone," cautioned the attendant.

"Can you find someone to act as a guide?" asked Harm.

"I'll see what I can do," promised the villager and he went into the office and got busy on the telephone.

"Willing to pay $15 for the horses and a guide?" he called after several minutes of phoning.

"Double that if necessary," replied Don.

"You'll have 'em in half an hour," replied the gasoline man. "I got Jim Greer out of bed and as soon as he woke up he said he'd take you in for $15. Of course, that's $15 a day and it may take you a couple of days to get in and back," chuckled the villager.

"How much of a start have Charlie Miller and the doctor?" asked Don.

"About three hours," was the reply. "They lost a lot of time getting their car stuck in the mud and having to come back for horses."

They arranged for the storage of their car, washed the mud off their hands and faces and then Don put in a long distance call for the office at Porter.

"Sorry," the operator told him, "but our lines are down in all directions now. I'll put it through as soon as possible."

"I can't wait," Don told her and he dictated a short message for her to put through as soon as the wire to Porter was patched up. Steve, Ed and the business manager would want to know that they had reached Akron and were going into the hills on horseback.

By the time Don completed his instructions to the operator, Jim Greer was outside with his horses. He swung down out of the saddle, a strapping, six foot two figure, a rubber blanket with a hole cut in the middle for his head, protecting him from the rain.

"Jim," said the station attendant, "here's the newspaper men who want to go to Phil Hunt's place. One of them says his uncle was on the plane that crashed this afternoon."

Jim Greer looked at Don and Harm in a strangely calculating manner as they introduced themselves.

"Come up from Porter through the storm?" he asked.

"Yes," replied Don.

"Then I guess you'll be able to stand the trip out to Hunt's," said Greer. He brought out a bundle he had carried under his blanket and unrolled two more large squares of rubber similar to the one he was wearing. They were lined on the inside and provided perfect protection for a man on horseback.

Don had ridden before but Harm was a greenhorn in the saddle and had to be boosted into the stirrups.

"This is going to be a tough night for me," he muttered, half to himself.

"Don't hold yourself stiff," advised Jim Greer. "You follow me and Durian will bring up the rear since he knows something about riding."

"Is there any chance of overtaking Charlie Miller and the doctor before they reach Hunt's?" asked Don.

"Not unless they've had some trouble," replied Greer. "Let's go. We've got about five hours of hard riding ahead of us."

He spoke to his horse and the little cavalcade, headed for the heart of the Indian hills, moved out into the storm.

Chapter III

THROUGH THE NIGHT

The lights of the village vanished in the wall of rain and there was only the sound of the storm, the dense blackness of the night and the steady plop-plop of the horses' hoofs as they sloshed through the mud.

The rubber blankets protected them and Don and Harm let their horses follow Jim Greer. Talk was impossible and with bowed heads they moved steadily forward. For an hour they rode in silence. Then Don felt his horse slowing its steady gait and he looked up. A shadowy form was just ahead of him.

"There's a trail running off here to the right," said Greer, "that will cut off four or five miles. The going is pretty rough but we'll tackle it if you say the word."

"Anything to make time," said Don.

Without another word Jim clucked to his horse. They turned off the road and onto a trail so dim that either Harm or Don would have lost it in the first hundred feet after they left the road, but Jim seemed to have almost uncanny eyesight.

Don noticed that the country was rougher and more densely wooded. They were getting into the hills. They had continued for another half hour when they heard a challenge from the darkness just ahead.

'Don't move!" warned Jim.

"What under the sun is happening?" Harm whispered to Don as they sat motionless on their horses.

"Haven't any idea," replied the managing editor.

A lantern appeared as if by magic and two men strode down the trail toward them. Harm and Don could see their guide a dozen paces ahead. His arms were held high above his head. Then they saw that the men approaching carried rifles.

The lantern was lifted and its rays fell on Jim Greer's face.

"Hello there, Jim," said one of the men who had stopped them. "What you doin' way up here tonight? Lucky we didn't take a pot shot at you."

"Hello Hank. Hello Abe," replied the guide. "An airplane crashed over near Phil Hunt's and I'm taking these newspaper men up there. One of 'em says his uncle was on the plane."

"Hadn't heard about no accident," replied the man Jim had addressed as Hank. "Was it pretty bad?"

"Seems as though," replied Jim. "If it's all right with you boys, we'll get moving along."

"Sure, go right ahead," replied Abe. "You won't have no trouble along the trail. We wouldn't have stopped you only there's been talk of federal men coming into the hills and we've got a big batch of mash cookin'."

"So long, boys," said Jim and he dug his heels into his horse.

"So long," they replied and stood to one side.

As Don and Harm rode by they lifted the lantern and gazed steadily at the young newspapermen. The lantern was shielded and Don and Harm could see nothing more than the outlines of two men, both tall and heavy. Then a shutter was snapped across the lantern and they were alone again.

Their guide didn't venture any further information on the incident and Don and Harm wouldn't stop him to ask questions for time was too valuable. When they had been in the saddle three hours Jim called a halt.

"There's a little valley just ahead with an old shack," he said. "We'll stop there and rest the horses. Fifteen minutes rest for them and some feed will save us time in the end."

The shack, a tumbledown structure with half of the roof fallen in, was sheltered by the dense foliage of a clump of towering oaks. Harm and Don were so stiff they could hardly get out of their saddles but they welcomed the opportunity to stretch their legs.

"I'll never be the same again," groaned Harm. "I'll have to eat my meals for the next week standing up."

"We're only a little over half way to Hunt's," chuckled Jim, who was greatly amused at Harm's complaints.

"Go ahead and let me stay here and die in peace," groaned the luckless reporter.

"The wolves might get you," warned Don.

"Don't kid me," replied Harm. "There isn't a wolf in this state."

"The hills are full of them," said Jim quietly. "I shot four of them last winter myself. They're big, gray timber wolves and when they get good and hungry they'll tackle anything."

"Let's hope they're not hungry tonight," said Harm.

"No need to worry at this time of year," continued the guide, "but they get pretty fierce in the winter."

Jim got three bags of oats from a roll at the back of his saddle and fastened a nosebag on each one of the horses. That task accomplished, he returned to the shelter of the shack and crouched down beside the boys.

"What was the idea of those fellows stopping us back there?" asked Harm.

"Just the Perkins brothers," replied Jim. "Like a lot of other folks in the hills they turn their corn into moonshine. They had a big batch in their still and with talk of federal men being around, didn't take any chances."

"You mean they stay out on the trail all night?"

"Sure," replied Jim. "There's four brothers all told and they take turns standing guard, two at a time. We

ran into Hank and Abe. This is a moonshine trail
but we'll get along all right unless somebody takes
a shot at us just on general principles."

"We'll hope for the best and probably get the worst,"
said Harm.

When the horses had finished their oats, Jim rolled
up the feed bags and fastened them back of his saddle.
Harm was so stiff it took the combined efforts of Jim
and Don to boost the reporter's 180 pounds into the
saddle, but they finally succeeded, much to the disgust
of Harm, who expressed a decided preference to the
shack and the company of a possible roaming timber
wolf.

"I'll never last the night out," he groaned as they
resumed their ride.

The trail went up one hill and down another for the
Indian hills were a portion of the state which had been
missed by the last advance of the glaciers into the
middle west. Where other parts had been levelled
by the last great ice sheet, the Indian hills escaped and
remained a ragged scar on the face of the prairie.
There was a wild beauty about them that was fascinat-
ing but they were also the home of a lawless clan which
found shelter in the hills and valleys.

The steady noise of the rain and the even movement
of his horse dulled Don's senses and his head dropped.
The next thing he knew was a sense of flying through

space and then a great splash as he landed in a puddle.

He cried out but there was no answer and he scrambled to his feet. His horse, which had stumbled and thrown him, was standing patiently, waiting for him to remount. Don bent down and felt the tendons of the animal's front legs. There appeared to be no sprain and he lifted himself into the saddle.

He spoke to the horse and they moved ahead. Then Don reined in sharply. He had lost Jim and Harm somehow. Which way should he turn? Left, right or straight ahead? The trail was too dim for anyone except an expert to follow, and he decided to wait and see if Jim and Harm would come back looking for him. At intervals he stood up in the stirrups and shouted but the night mocked him as his cries went unanswered.

Don was about to dismount and attempt to find and follow the trail on foot when he heard a faint cry. He shouted a reply and five minutes later heard the horses of Jim and Harm splashing toward him.

Harm pressed forward and was the first to reach Don's side. "Anything wrong?" he asked. "We were scared silly when we missed you."

"I'm a little wet and muddy and scared," admitted Don. "I was dozing when my horse stumbled and the next thing I knew I was being the big splash in a mud puddle."

"I was dozing, too," admitted Harm, "or I'd have missed you right away. We must have gone on a half a mile before Jim stopped for a short rest and then we missed you."

"We've lost fifteen or twenty minutes," said Jim quietly. "Keep awake after this and yell if you fall off your horse."

Before Don could reply, Jim swung his horse around and they resumed their journey. They came to the end of the moonshine trail and turned onto a narrow, rutted road. There was danger of a horse stumbling in the ruts and breaking a leg so Jim guided his little party along the edge.

They rode for miles in silence and every bone in Don's body ached with fatigue. The night was growing colder and he beat his arms together to keep up the circulation. He could well imagine the agonies the inexperienced Harm was going through for five hours in a saddle on such a night was enough for a veteran horseman.

Don wondered what time it was. They had left Akron a few minutes before ten and Jim had said it would be a good five hour ride. Must be well after midnight. He pulled out his watch but it was too dark to distinguish the hands.

They jogged steadily onward, a silent, determined little cavalcade. The rain eased off into a cold, steady

drizzle and the dampness chilled them to the bone.
Don kept moving in his saddle but even that failed
to warm him.

When a light finally showed through the darkness
ahead he shouted to Harm and Jim and kicked his
horse into a trot. He splashed alongside the guide.

"Is that Hunt's place ahead?" he cried.

"Yep," replied the stolid Jim. "'Nother five minutes
and we'll be there."

Harm ached too much to talk and he could only
nod his head at the good news.

The door of the house opened and a shaft of golden
light streamed out. There was the whinny of a horse
and Jim's animal lifted its head and answered.

They could see men moving around outside the
house now.

"Looks like Charlie Miller and Doc Hanson just
got in," said Jim.

The guide was right in his surmise and when they
reached the Hunt farmyard they were greeted by the
doctor and the editor of the *Akron Weekly Argus*.

Jim introduced Don and Harm and Charlie Miller
and the doctor welcomed them cordially.

"What time did you start?" the doctor asked Jim.

"Right around ten," replied the guide, "but we took
the short cut through the hills. Pretty rough going
but it saved time. Uncle of one of the boys here is

supposed to be aboard the plane and they were anxious to get here as soon as possible."

Mrs. Hunt came to the door of the farmhouse.

"I'll have plenty of hot water ready when you come back, doctor," she called.

"Was your uncle the pilot?" Doctor Hanson asked Don.

"No," he replied. "He's Robert Durian, publisher of the *Porter Press*. He telegraphed that he was leaving Beldon on the afternoon air express and his name was the only one on the passenger list which the aviation company had."

"That's strange," said Charlie Miller. "Mrs. Hunt told us there was only one man in the plane. He was the pilot."

Chapter IV

SEALED LIPS

The young managing editor of the *Press* wheeled around and seized his correspondent's shoulders.

"What's that?" he cried.

"I said Mrs. Hunt told us there was only one man in the plane and that he was the pilot," repeated Charlie Miller.

"But there must be more than one," insisted Don. "My uncle telegraphed he was leaving Beldon on the afternoon plane and the passenger report of the company showed he was aboard the ship when it started for Porter."

"Let's go in the house and talk to the pilot," suggested Harm.

"He isn't there," replied Charlie Miller. "Phil Hunt couldn't get him out of the wreckage of the plane. Phil's stayed up in the hills through all the storm."

Don hesitated to ask the next question, but it must be asked.

"Is, is he dead?"

"Can't say," replied Doctor Hanson. "Mrs. Hunt says he must be hurt pretty badly. We're going on at once. Better come along for we may need you to help bring him back."

Harm was so stiff they had to again boost him into
the saddle but he insisted on continuing the trip to
the scene of the plane wreck. Charlie Miller, who had
often hunted on the farm, led the way out of the
barnyard. The light in the house faded into the storm
and their horses sloshed through the mud and water.

For fifteen minutes they moved ahead through the
steady drizzle before Don saw the gleam of a lantern
ahead. They threaded their way through a clump
of trees and came out into a small clearing. On the
far side they saw a tangled heap of wreckage, all that
remained of the once proud air liner.

Don kicked his horse into a trot and bounced across
the field. Phil Hunt, lantern in hand, was crawling
from the wreckage.

"Doctor with you?" he asked.

"Yes," replied Don, "he's right behind."

"Good thing," replied the farmer. "The fellow is
getting weaker all the time."

"But are you sure there was only one man in the
plane?" Don asked.

"Yep," was the quick reply. "If there was more
they must have jumped out before the crash for I've
looked all around the clearing and into the timber."

Doctor Hanson, Charlie Miller and Jim Greer arrived and dismounted. Harm was struggling along
somewhere in the rear.

"You'll have to crawl into the wreckage, doctor," said Phil Hunt. "Better follow me."

The farmer ducked under the crumpled framework of the right wing and crawled into what remained of the cabin. Jammed in the front end was the body of Carl Bain, veteran pilot of the air express. The center section of the wing had caught and held him secure. Possibly it had saved his life at the moment of the crash but now it threatened to hold him fast while his life ebbed away through exposure and his injuries.

"Can't get in close enough to see how badly he's hurt," said Doctor Hanson. "I'll stay inside and you fellows get out and see if you can lift up the framework of this wing."

Phil Hunt, Charlie Miller, Jim and Don crawled out of the cabin to find that Harm had finally arrived.

"Somebody help me out of this saddle," he implored. "I'm so stiff I can't even lift my feet out of the stirrups."

They boosted him down and then went around to the front of the plane. It was a single-engined monoplane and the left half of the wing had been snapped off close to the fuselage. Part of the center section had been jammed down and it was under this that the pilot lay helpless.

"If we all get hold of this stub left end," said Don, "we may be able to straighten it up enough to let Doctor Hanson pull him out."

"We'll give it a try," agreed Charlie Miller.

They got down under the stub of the wing, looking for all the world like linemen on a football team ready to spring into the line of scrimmage.

"Let's go!" cried Charlie Miller. They braced themselves and thrust their shoulders upward.

The wreckage creaked and groaned. Don's muscles ached from the terrific strain of the lift and Harm, already stiff and sore from his long ride, groaned aloud as he pushed upward on the wing. They felt the wing start to give and then heard it snap as it came free.

"Hold it up," cried Doctor Hanson from inside the plane. "I'll have him out in less than a minute."

The men held the wing on their shoulders while the doctor worked to free the pilot. The rain kept up its ceaseless whisper on the torn canvas of the plane.

Don was thinking rapidly. There appeared to be no question about it now. His uncle had not been on the afternoon express when it crashed. What, then, had happened to him? Had he changed his plans before the plane left Beldon? But if he had done that, reasoned Don, the passenger list given out by the aviation company would not have contained his uncle's name. It was all a puzzling muddle and it now looked as though the pilot was the only man who would be able to clear up the mystery that night.

"Let it drop," said Doctor Hanson and they heard him dragging the pilot out of the cabin.

When they reached the other side of the plane, the doctor had the pilot stretched on the ground. The lantern flickered crazily and it was difficult for the doctor to make much of an examination.

"Head injuries," he murmured. "Probably a fracture of the skull but it may not prove fatal."

He started to open the pilot's blouse when the lantern wavered and went out.

"Who's got a match?" asked Charlie Miller as he bent down and fumbled for the lantern.

"Match won't do any good," replied Phil Hunt. "It's out of oil."

"That's a fine thing to have happen now," snorted Doctor Hanson.

"Come on," he added. "We've got to get this man into a house. One of you take off your rubber blanket. We can carry him in that."

Don started to strip off his garment but Jim Greer was ahead of him. They put the heavy blanket on the ground, laid the flyer on it, and then took up the slow march to the farmhouse.

Doctor Hanson, Jim, Charlie Miller and Don each took a corner of the blanket. Phil Hunt walked just ahead to lead the way and Harm, leading the horses, followed.

They were forced to rest every five minutes and it took them nearly half an hour before they reached the farmhouse. Once or twice the unconscious airman groaned and Doctor Hanson urged them to make all possible speed.

Mrs. Hunt was waiting in the doorway for them and had made up a bed on the couch in the living room. A white porcelain basin of steaming hot water and a stack of clean towels were on a chair beside the couch.

Doctor Hanson stripped off his raincoat and gloves and sat down beside the flyer. For the first time Don had a really good look at Bain the veteran pilot of the air express and he was surprised at his age. He couldn't be more than 29 or 30, tall, with broad shoulders and a mop of light hair that now was matted with blood from a sharp cut on his head. His face was strangely pale, his lips were blue and he was breathing softly.

The doctor worked rapidly, cutting away the flyer's clothing with a pair of surgical scissors that flashed coldly in the warm rays of the kerosene lamp.

The shirt and the jersey underwear beneath the heavy suede jacket were stiff with dried blood and Doctor Hanson shook his head.

"Can't feel any rib fractures," he muttered, "yet he's lost a lot of blood."

The scissors flashed again; then stopped suddenly as Doctor Hanson bent forward. When he straightened up his face was almost as white as that of the man on the couch.

"Good heavens," he exclaimed. "This man has been shot. It's murder!"

Chapter V

THE SECOND PASSENGER

The little group in the living room looked at the doctor with unbelieving eyes.

"I tell you he's been shot," repeated Doctor Hanson. "It looks like attempted murder."

"It can't be," protested Harm, "for there was no one else on the plane when it crashed."

"Then you explain this," replied Doctor Hanson and he pointed to a bullet wound well down on the left side of the flyer's body.

"This man was shot from behind," asserted the doctor, "and you can't make me believe for one minute that the pilot of a cross-state air express goes around shooting himself like that and crashing his plane just for fun."

"Of course not," agreed Don, "and this certainly adds another perplexing angle to the events of the day. First my uncle starts for Porter on the Beldon-Porter plane, then the plane crashes here, the pilot is found but no trace of my uncle and now we learn that there has evidently been an attempt to murder the pilot."

"Pretty nearly successful, I'd say," added Charlie Miller.

"Not if I have any luck," retorted Doctor Hanson,

who was busy caring for the flyer's wounds. "The exposure and loss of blood are serious but he looks young and husky and unless there are complications he may pull through."

"How long before he'll be able to talk?" asked Don.

"Hard to say," replied the doctor. "He may be able to say a few words tomorrow. Perhaps it will be a week. Never can tell."

"In the meantime, we'll have to guess at what happened above the clouds," said Harm.

Mrs. Hunt came in to announce that she had a lunch ready in the kitchen. All except the doctor answered her invitation and she brought his lunch in to him.

Mrs. Hunt was a kindly, pleasant little woman, who bustled about her kitchen making sure that there was plenty for everyone. There was steaming hot coffee for those who wanted it and for others cool glasses of milk. A platter of bacon and eggs disappeared and another took its place.

"I'm sorry I haven't beds for everyone," apologized Mrs. Hunt, "but we only have the one bedroom."

"Oh, that's all right," chuckled Jim Greer. "We'll just go out in the barn and bed down in the hay. I expect these men are about ready for a little sleep."

"There's nothing more we can do until daylight," said Don, "and then I want to go back to the plane. We may find something interesting there."

They thanked Mrs. Hunt for the lunch and then splashed through the mud puddles in the farmyard to the barn.

Jeff led the way up the ladder to the haymow and they spread their rubber blankets, inside out, upon the clean, sweet-smelling hay.

Harm, who had suffered more than Don on the trip, was the first to fall asleep. Then Charlie Miller and Jim Greer followed and Don alone remained awake. His mind was unusually clear despite the great fatigue which his body felt. He must think, must review the events of the day and plan his next step.

What had become of his uncle? He must have left Beldon on the plane since his message and the airplane company's passenger list had indicated this. What, then, had happened between the time the plane left its western terminal and the moment it crashed in the Indian hills?

When Don awoke the sun was streaming through the single large window of the haymow and the other members of the party were moving around. He looked at his watch and sat up suddenly. It was eight o'clock. They should have been up and on their way to the scene of the wreck long before but the fatigue of the past night's events had worn even Jim Greer down.

Harm, who had suffered agonies jouncing around in the saddle on their long ride into the hills, had to be pulled out of the hay but once on his feet, declared he was ready for anything that happened.

"We'll take a look in Mrs. Hunt's kitchen," said Charlie Miller, "and see what's on the table."

Then found Doctor Hanson at breakfast and the genial country physician smiled as they came in.

"Good news, boys," he said. "It looks now like our aviator friend is going to get well. He won't be able to talk for days but I'm confident he'll pull through."

"Glad to hear that," replied Don, "but the fact that he won't be in shape to talk for some time means that we'll have to grope for the solution as to what happened in the air yesterday."

"Telephone line repaired yet, Mrs. Hunt?" asked Charlie Miller.

"Not yet," replied the farmer's wife.

"Then how are we going to get our stories back to the office in time for the editions this afternoon?" asked Harm.

"Looks like we'll have to send someone back to Akron on horseback," said Don.

"Count me out," groaned Harm.

"Jim's the logical one to make the trip," suggested Charlie Miller. "He knows every inch of the hills and can ride twice as fast as any of the rest."

The guide, his mouth filled with a doughnut, waggled his head, indicating that he was ready.

Don turned to Mrs. Hunt.

"If you'll loan us a few sheets of paper, we'll write our stories and send them back with Jim."

The paper was forthcoming and Don and Harm shoved their plates aside and bent to the task of writing the story of the disappearance of Robert Durian, publisher of the *Press*, the attempted murder of the pilot and the crash of the afternoon air express.

They wrote feverishly for half an hour, Don handling the straight news story of the accident and Harm writing a flashing feature story, describing the valley in which the crash had occurred, the long ride through the night to reach the scene and the discovery that there had been an attempt to murder Carl Bain, the pilot.

While Don and Harm were going over their stories, Jim Greer saddled his horse and brought it around to the door of the farmhouse. It was just nine o'clock when they handed the scrawled pages of manuscript to him to take back to Akron and telephone to the *Press*.

"If you can't get through by telephone," said Don, "take the stories down to the depot at Akron. The railroad people will be glad to send them on their train order wires if there isn't any other way."

"I'll get them through," promised Jim. He tucked the stories inside his jacket, gave his hat a jerk to set it firmly on his head and started the long trip to Akron.

They watched his horse splatter through the mud of the farmyard and turn onto the narrow road that led out of the hills. In less than five minutes the rider disappeared in the timber and the newspaper men planned their campaign for the day.

"Let's get back to the plane," said Don. "I'm not fully satisfied that Uncle Robert wasn't on board when it crashed. The plane might have bumped several times before it finally came to rest."

They decided to leave their horses at the Hunt farm and proceeded on foot. With the September air crisp and invigorating, the sun was rapidly drying the ground and they reached the clearing which held the remains of the air express in a little less than half an hour.

The plane was about as completely wrecked as anything Don or Harm had ever seen and Charlie Miller whistled in open astonishment.

"I can't figure out how that pilot ever lived," he said.

"There must be a special providence that looks after aviators," said Harm quietly.

The terrific impact had smashed the long nose of the plane back into the cabin, crumpled the landing gear and reduced the once proud sky queen into little more than a tangled pile of steel tubing and sagging linen.

Don crawled under one wing and through the

smashed door into the cabin. The ship had been a six passenger monoplane. The seats had been smashed in the crash but by some miracle magazines in the rack at one side were still in their place.

While Harm and Charlie Miller made a thorough search outside the plane and around the clearing, Don went over the cabin inch by inch. After half an hour of painstaking work he was forced to admit that he had failed to gain any additional information. There was nothing to indicate that his uncle had been aboard the air express when it roared out of the sky out of control.

Don backed out of the cabin and stood up to stretch his cramped muscles when he saw the door of the baggage compartment, just back of the passenger cabin, ajar.

The managing editor of the *Press* opened the door and peered inside the compartment. There were several objects in the section toward the tail of the plane and he pulled them out.

The first was a black-leather traveling bag. There was an identification tag on the handle but Don recognized that piece of luggage instantly. It belonged to his uncle! It was the bag the publisher of the *Press* had carried when he left the office earlier in the week on the trip which had resulted in his mysterious disappearance.

Don shouted to Harm and Charlie Miller, who came on the run.

"What's up?" demanded Harm as he arrived, breathless.

Don pointed to the luggage.

"I've found Uncle Robert's traveling bag," he explained, "which clears up any doubt of whether he was aboard the plane when it left Beldon."

"Looks that way," admitted Charlie Miller, "but it doesn't tell us what happened between the time the plane left Beldon and when it crashed here."

"Perhaps something in the bag will tell us why Uncle Robert went on this mysterious trip," said Don as he bent down to open it.

The case was locked and it defied Don's efforts to force the lock. Charlie Miller hunted around until he found several good sized rocks. Placing one back of the lock, he used the other to batter it to pieces.

Don opened the traveling bag, the contents of which were still neatly packed. He pulled out pajamas, a clean shirt and one soiled one, his uncle's shaving kit, several pairs of socks and handkerchiefs and a railroad time table.

"Is that all?" asked Harm, who was trying to peer over Don's shoulder.

"Every last thing," admitted Don as he picked up the traveling bag, turned it upside down and shook it in the forlorn hope that he might have overlooked some scrap of paper that would help them.

"Let's have a look at this other bag," suggested Harm and they turned their attention to the second piece of luggage which Don had found in the baggage compartment. It was a cheap, brown imitation leather suitcase, locked, but with the key dangling on a string from the handle. There was no tag on it for identification.

"Can't tell whether it's your uncle's," said Harm.

"Go ahead and open it," said Charlie Miller. "I'm a deputy sheriff of this county and if anyone objects later I'll tell 'em it was in the line of duty investigating the attempted murder of Pilot Bain."

Don bent down, unlocked the brown suitcase and opened it. With unbelieving eyes they stared at its contents. The suitcase was filled with nothing more than old newspapers, crumpled and stuffed into the traveling case.

"Now what do you make of that?" demanded Harm.

"It's all getting too deep for your Uncle Charlie," admitted the editor of the *Akron Weekly Argus*. "So many things have happened in the last twenty-four hours I'd better be getting back to my office before I go completely batty."

"There is some significance to this suitcase," said Don, "for people don't have suitcases aboard an air express for no reason at all, especially a suitcase filled with old newspapers." Harm got down on his knees and started rummaging through the papers.

"Most of these are issues of the *Beldon Bulletin* earlier in the week," he said. "Here's a copy of Monday's edition and another one is the Tuesday's paper."

Charlie Miller started to examine the outside of the case when Don stopped him.

"Better not get any more fingerprints on it than necessary," he explained. "We'll take this suitcase and Uncle Robert's traveling bag back to Porter with us and get a fingerprint expert on the job. He may be able to give us a little light on this mystery."

"Fine idea," agreed the editor of the *Akron Argus.* "You boys aren't missing any bets and I'll venture you get to the bottom of this thing if anyone can."

"We'll do our best," said Harm quietly.

"Which," added the editor of the weekly, "is mighty good if I'm any judge of newspapermen."

They took the papers out of the suitcase one by one, smoothed them out and went over each page carefully in the hope that there might be some item which would be helpful. They were about to give it up as a hopeless task when Harm found a short story on one of the inside pages.

"Here's a couple of paragraphs about your uncle," he said. "Listen to this:

"'Mr. Robert Durian, editor and publisher of the *Porter Press*, is in Beldon this week where he has been visiting his old friend, George Huckins, former warden of the state prison. Mr. Durian and Mr. Huckins were classmates in college and have been renewing acquaintance. Mr. Durian plans to return to Porter tomorrow, and will probably take the afternoon cross-state air express.'"

"That explains why your uncle was in Beldon," continued Harm.

"At least it gives us a clue as to who he visited," agreed Don. "He's mentioned former Warden Huckins a number of times and I knew they were in college together. We'll get in touch with him as soon as we can get to a telephone that isn't out of commission."

"Notice anything strange about this page?" asked Charlie Miller.

Don examined the page which contained the short story about his uncle's visit in Beldon.

"It looks pretty well thumb-marked and dirty," he said.

"Like somebody had been mighty interested in something on the page," persisted the editor of the *Akron Argus*.

"Yes," agreed Don.

"Then notice how soiled it is around the story about your uncle. Appears to me someone was awfully anxious about what he was doing. They must have read it three or four times from the looks of the page."

"I believe you're right," exclaimed Don. "We're making a little progress and as soon as we can get in touch with Mr. Huckins in Beldon we ought to make a whole lot more."

"Then you don't think your uncle was in the plane when it crashed?" asked Harm.

Don was silent for several moments.

"No," he said slowly, "I don't think so. There isn't any question but what he was aboard when the ship left Beldon but there is a possibility that the pilot landed before he reached here. Perhaps it was at Uncle Robert's direction or for some other reason."

"But he wouldn't disappear without leaving some message," insisted Harm. "He'd realize how much you and the entire office would worry."

"That's just what's troubling me," said Don. "Uncle Robert wouldn't willingly disappear without some word. The only other explanation is a forced disappearance. I may be playing a foolish hunch, but before this mystery is solved I think the lid's going to blow off the political pot in this part of the state and when it does, Marcus Krieg, mayor of Porter, is going to drop into the pot."

"And while you're summing up things," put in Harm, "don't forget there will be a murder charge against the man who attempted to kill Pilot Bain."

They replaced the newspapers in the brown suitcase and closed it carefully, lest they smudge any possible fingerprints on the outside. That done, Don repacked his uncle's belongings and they started back to the Hunt farm.

"I'm satisfied in my own mind that Uncle Robert wasn't on board the ship when it crashed," Don told Charlie Miller, "but to make sure, I want a searching party organized to comb the hills near here."

"Jim Greer is just the man to handle that job," replied the editor of the Akron paper. "He'll be able to round up a dozen of these hill people and they can comb the country. Course they'll expect to be paid."

"Certainly," agreed Don. "I'll arrange with Jim when he returns."

They reached the Hunt farm just as a large truck lumbered into the farmyard. Half a dozen people were in the machine and the first one out was Tony Marlas, manager of the airport at Porter.

"How bad was it?" demanded the excited little field manager.

"Didn't you meet a man on horseback carrying our stories into town?" asked Don.

"Haven't met a soul since we left Akron," said Marlas. "We've ploughed through mud for hours.

I've got a couple of nurses with me and stretchers for the injured."

Doctor Hanson, who had remained at the farm, stepped up.

"Pilot Bain is resting quietly now," he said, "but I wouldn't advise moving him until he regains consciousness. Mrs. Hunt has turned over a room for him and the nurses can remain and care for him here."

"How about your uncle?" Tony asked Don. "I hope, I hope, it wasn't bad."

"That's something I can't answer, Tony," replied Don, "for when we reached the plane we couldn't find him. We've searched again this morning but the only thing we found was his traveling bag."

"Then how about the other passenger?" asked the airport manager.

"What other passenger?" exclaimed Don.

"The passenger list which came through by radiophone from Beldon yesterday was garbled," explained the airport manager. "There were three aboard the plane when it departed, Pilot Carl Bain, your uncle and a third man who was listed as Otto Bauer."

"There was only one man in the wreckage," said Don significantly, "and he was Pilot Bain."

Chapter VI

DANGER AHEAD

The revelation that there had been a second passenger aboard the afternoon air express when it left Beldon brought a new and even more baffling angle into the mystery. Just what part had this third man played in the events which had led to the disappearance of Don's uncle, the attempted murder of Pilot Bain, and the crashing of the plane?

It was a question that Don refused even to attempt to answer and instead of wasting time over trying to figure it out, he set into motion a machine designed to pick up every possible clue in connection with the mystery.

The nurses were left on duty at the Hunt home and Doctor Hanson, Charlie Miller, Harm and Don prepared to return to Akron in the truck with Tony Marlas and the mechanics he had brought from the field at Porter.

"Nothing we can do about the wreck of the plane right now," concluded Tony. "If Pilot Bain dies the coroner in this county will want to go over it for evidence and there isn't enough left for salvage."

The heavy machine lumbered out of the farmyard and creaked its way over the narrow road. Mile after mile they rumbled along, seldom seeing even a sign of habitation, and even then the rude houses appeared deserted. But the country was in the height of its beauty. The hills were covered with a heavy growth of timber, peaks of which had been touched with the magic color that only the early frosts can bring out in the foliage.

They were half way to Akron in mid-afternoon when they met Jim Greer returning on horseback. The truck creaked to a stop and Jim brought his horse up beside them.

"Get the stories through?" asked Don.

"Yep," was the terse reply. "The phone wires had just been patched up when I reached town."

"I'll bet Steve was glad to hear from us," said Harm, for he could imagine the city editor's impatience at the delay in the stories about the accident.

"He appeared to be a mite excited," admitted Jim with a slow grin that extended clear across his face.

Don explained the recent developments in the hills and Jim agreed to get together a searching party to comb the country for some possible trace of the missing publisher of the *Porter Press*.

"There's just a chance," went on Don, "that the plane may have landed in some valley and taken off without my uncle. I'm positive that the second passenger, Otto Bauer, had an important part in this disappearance."

Jim promised to telephone any news to the office at Porter and they parted company, the truck continuing its journey to Akron and the lone horseman jogging slowly into the heart of the hills.

They reached Akron just before sundown and Don and Harm made final arrangements with Charlie Mil ler before starting the drive back to Porter.

"I'll keep my ear to the ground," promised the country editor, "and telephone anything I learn."

"Do that," urged Don, "for unless I'm playing a mighty poor hunch, the whole secret of this mystery is somewhere out in the hills."

"Then why not stay here until we can run it to ground?" asked Harm.

"Perhaps it is right under our nose and we're too close," smiled Don.

"No, Harm," he continued, "we've got a lot of work to do at Porter. Don't forget the campaign against the mayor which must be carried on no matter what happens. Then we've got to send someone to Beldon to check up on George Huckins and find out why Uncle Robert visited the former warden of the state prison. When we've learned that we may know more about his disappearance."

They said goodbye to Charlie Miller, climbed into the coupe which was waiting for them, and roared away in the twilight on their seventy mile trip to Porter.

Don, who was driving, kept a close watch on the road. He was so physically tired that he was afraid of dozing and losing control of the car. When they reached the valley of the Coon river, flares on the road warned them of danger ahead and they crept through the purple of the early night.

The approach at the west end of the bridge had been washed away but a temporary affair of timber had been constructed by the maintenance crew and they moved over it onto the main span of the bridge. The river was still high and they could see its swirling, black waters, but it was not running over the road and they picked up speed rapidly after leaving the bridge.

Half way to Porter Don stopped the car and roused Harm, who had slept ever since they left the valley of the Coon.

"You'll have to take the wheel," he told him. "I'm so sleepy I'll put us in the ditch if I go another mile."

Harm rubbed the sleep from his eyes and they exchanged places. Don was sound asleep almost before Harm finished shifting gears and getting the coupe into high speed. The next thing he knew was when Harm shook him and informed him they were home.

They parked the car in front of the apartment building and went up in the elevator. For a moment Don forgot the baffling mystery which confronted him as he thought how restful it would be to take a shower and get into clean, fresh clothes.

When they stepped into their apartment-home Steve and Ed were waiting for them and back in one corner, slouched in an easy chair, was Harvey Hendricks, the business manager.

"We want to hear the whole story," said Ed McGuire after the first greetings were over. "What happened in the hills?"

"The details can wait," insisted Steve. "Can't you see Don and Harm are about all in. After they have a shower and get into some clean clothes they'll feel more like talking."

"I vote in favor of Steve's suggestion," put in the business manager. "We want to hear everything in detail but you'll be able to talk a lot better after you've relaxed a little."

Don and Harm welcomed the plan and while they were relaxing under the shower, Ed and Steve busied themselves getting a hot lunch. When Don and Harm returned to the living room, the appetizing odor of bacon and eggs was floating out of the kitchenette.

"Believe me, that smells good," exclaimed Harm. "Climbing around in the hills and riding horseback half the night just about finished me. I don't think I'll ever be able to sit down comfortably again."

"Grub's on," Steve called from the dining alcove and they gathered around the table. The lunch was simple but there was an abundance of crisp bacon and eggs.

"Everybody pull up a chair and help themselves," he urged and even the business manager, who explained that he had eaten only a short time before, succumbed to bacon and eggs.

Steve got two quarts of milk from the ice chest and filled large glasses with the ice-cold liquid.

"This will put new energy into you," he advised Don and Harm.

"I feel a hundred per cent better right now," grinned Don. "Now what do you want to know about the Indian hills mystery?"

"Everything," insisted Steve. "We've been sitting on pins and needles ever since you and Harm left. You're usually so prompt in getting a story back to the office that I just about went crazy before the guide telephoned the story from Akron. He didn't waste any words but I gathered you'd had a hard time getting into the hills and then couldn't reach a phone to send the story back."

"There was a phone within reach," commented Harm, "but that's all the good it was. The line to Akron was down and we had to send our stories back by the guide and it's better than twenty miles on horseback."

Don explained every detail of their drive to Akron and of the long trip to the Hunt farm. With graphic description he told them of the finding of the wreck and the revelation by Doctor Hanson that there had been an attempt to murder the pilot.

"Didn't you find a trace of your uncle?" asked the business manager anxiously.

"We found his traveling bag in the baggage compartment of the plane," said Don, "but I'm positive he wasn't aboard the ship when it crashed. Neither was the other passenger."

"What other passenger?" demanded Steve.

The young managing editor of the *Press* told how the passenger list had been garbled the day before in transmission and that two men had been aboard in addition to Pilot Bain when the plane left Beldon.

"And there was no trace of this Otto Bauer?" asked Ed.

"No more than of Uncle Robert," admitted Don. "We found another suitcase and brought it back with us to have a complete check made of any possible fingerprints. What I want to do tonight is to plan a complete campaign which I hope will shed new light on Uncle Robert's disappearance and the attempted murder of Pilot Bain."

Don went on further to explain that they had examined the contents of the suitcase and found the thumb-marked page with the story of his uncle's visit to Beldon.

"I want someone to get the first train for Beldon,"

he said, "and see George Huckins at once. It's too dangerous to telephone or telegraph for our plans might leak."

"Let me go," said Ed. "That's just my line of stuff. I'll find out what time I can get a train for Beldon."

The police reporter stepped to the telephone and called the union station.

"There's a westbound train at midnight that will get me into Beldon in the morning," he said. "How about taking that?"

"The sooner the better," agreed Don and Ed made a Pullman reservation for the midnight train.

With Ed selected to make the trip to Beldon, Don turned his attention to the campaign against the mayor.

"What were you able to do today," he asked the city editor.

"Not a whole lot," admitted Steve. "The mayor's clamped the lid down tight and we can't even get into the offices at the city hall to interview city officials. Even when we meet them on the street they don't dare talk to us. Ed reported at noon that word had gone out around town that the days of the *Press* are numbered and I wasn't able to scare the state labor department into ordering an investigation of the gas plant explosion. The mayor's been tightening his political fences with the governor and it looks like we're out of luck on the explosion."

"Keep hammering away at every opportunity," said Don. "Our first task now is to find Uncle Robert and get him back here safely. Unless I'm way off the track, his disappearance is linked with the attack by Mayor Krieg."

"I've had the same feeling all along," said the business manager. "I've supported your uncle all the way on his fight against the mayor but unless you find him and find him soon we may be licked."

"What do you mean by that?" asked Don.

"Mayor Krieg has obtained a $100,000 note against the paper and is calling for payment a week from Saturday. That means we have just eight days in which to find your uncle and get him back here."

"But how could he get a note for that amount?" asked Don.

"We've been running behind for the last two months," explained the business manager. "Summer is always a light time for us and annually we borrow a large sum from local bankers to tide us over this part of the year. We did it this summer and after your uncle disappeared, Krieg bought the note and notified me this afternoon that he would demand payment a week from Saturday."

"Can't you get outside bankers to take it up?" asked Steve.

"Not if local bankers won't provide the funds and

you know as well as I do that Krieg would put a stop
to that. Our only chance is to find Don's uncle. He
has personal securities more than ample to protect the
note but we can't get at them unless we have his
personal authorization and we've got to find him before we can get that."

"Then if we don't find Uncle Robert before a week
from Saturday the *Press* will pass into the control of
Marcus Krieg?" demanded Don.

"I'm sorry," said the business manager, "but that's
just what will happen."

Chapter VII

A MYSTERIOUS ATTACK

The business manager's startling statement that the *Press* might fall into the hands of Mayor Krieg, publisher of the rival *Midwest News,* left the group of young newspapermen speechless. Don was the first to recover and when he spoke again it was with his customary determination and calmness.

"We'll work all the harder to find Uncle Robert," he said, "and it means we can't afford to ignore a single possibility."

"Ed," he continued, "while you're in Beldon talking with George Huckins make every effort to find out all you can about Otto Bauer, who he is, what he does and why he took the afternoon air express on Thursday."

"I'll go over that town with a fine-toothed comb," promised the police reporter. "I know the city editor of the Beldon paper and he'll help me if I get up against a blank wall."

"There's another thing we've almost forgotten," put in Harm. "The traveling bag and suitcase we found in the wreckage of the plane are still in the rear compartment of the coupe. We'd better take them to a fingerprint expert."

"You're right," agreed Don.

Turning to Ed, he asked:

"Will the expert at the police department do the work for us?"

"I expect he'd do it all right," said Ed, "but you can be sure that he would send a set of the prints to the mayor."

"Which," agreed Don, "is just what we don't want to happen."

"How about Professor Duer, the criminologist at the university?" asked the business manager.

"Splendid suggestion," said Don. "It's getting late but I don't suppose he'll object to being disturbed even at this hour. We've done a good many favors for him and he's one man on whom we can rely."

Professor Duer was finally located in his laboratory in the chemistry building at the university and Don explained the purpose of his call.

"I'll be delighted to assist you," said the noted criminologist. "When can you bring the bags over?"

"Either tonight or the first thing in the morning."

"You might as well come tonight," said Professor Duer. "I've an experiment under way that will keep me in my laboratory most of the night and I can work on the fingerprints on the bags if I have them here. I take it that you are anxious to have my findings as soon as possible."

"We are mighty anxious," admitted Don. "I'll bring the bags over within the hour. Thank you so much, professor."

"Not at all, not at all," replied the criminologist. "It will be but a small return of the many favors your uncle and your paper have done for me. Ring the buzzer on the main door of the building and I'll come down and let you in."

Ed, who had been packing a few necessities in a traveling bag for his trip to Beldon, came out of the dressing room he shared with Harm.

"How about someone giving me a ride to the station?" he inquired. "There's also the ever-present need for shekels."

The business manager grinned and dug into one pocket, producing a thick roll of currency.

"That remark was aimed at me," he chuckled. "How much will you need for your trip?"

"A hundred dollars ought to be enough," replied Ed. Then as he eyed the business manager's handful of bills, he added, "Well, maybe you'd better make it a hundred and fifty or two hundred. Then I won't have to wire you collect for more cash."

"We'll compromise with a hundred and fifty," decided the business manager, "and if you wire for more money we'll leave you stranded in Beldon."

Harvey Hendricks put on his topcoat to leave.

"No need of my going to the train," said the business manager, "so I'll run along home."

"No thanks," he continued as Don offered to take him in the car. "It's only a few blocks and a brisk walk before going to bed will do me good. Good luck, Ed, and goodnight."

"Goodnight," they replied as the business manager left the apartment.

Ten minutes later Don and Ed started for the union station where the police reporter was to take the midnight train for Beldon.

They descended to the main floor in the automatic elevator and walked through the dimly lighted lobby. In the street outside a single light struggled to dispel the gloom. The coupe Don and Harm had used on their trip into the Indian hills kept a lonely vigil beyond the lamplight.

They had almost reached the car when Ed grabbed Don by one arm.

"Wait!" he whispered. "Listen!"

Don stopped instantly. What could Ed have heard? Blocks away there was the voice of the city where life still throbbed along the main arteries of travel but here on the side street everything was calm and dark.

"I don't hear anything," he protested.

"I thought I heard someone groan," said Ed, "but it might have been something else."

Don started toward the car, only to stop as suddenly as had Ed. There was no question now in the mind of either newspaperman. Someone had moaned as, though severely injured.

"It came from the other side of the car," said Ed as he ran into the street with Don at his heels.

Beside the left front wheel of their coupe they discerned a deeper shadow as though something or someone had been dropped there with little ceremony.

"Give me a hand," directed Don. "Someone must have been struck by a 'hit and run' driver and left here in the street. We'll get him over to the light and see how badly he's hurt."

Ed bent to the task and the newspapermen carried the unconscious pedestrian toward the entrance of the apartment house. They were almost there when Ed caught a full view of the injured man's face.

"Don," he cried, "it's Harvey Hendricks, the business manager!"

The managing editor stopped and looked down at the pale face.

"You're right, Ed," he agreed. "We'll take him into the lobby and see what we can do."

They availed themselves of a large settee in the lobby and the business manager was made as comfortable as possible.

"This doesn't look like a 'hit and run' driver to me,"

said Ed. "Someone must have clouted him over the head with a blackjack or a heavy club."

"His pulse is steady and he doesn't seem to have lost any blood," said Don. "I believe he'll come around in a minute or two."

Ed hurried away, to return a minute later with a handkerchief which he had soaked in cold water. He applied this to the business manager's forehead and moistened the dry lips.

Hendricks groaned several times and mumbled to himself before he opened his eyes. When he did he recognized Don and sank back on the settee with a sigh of relief. It was ten minutes more before he was able to sit up and tell them what had happened. His first words were a question.

"Are the bags in your car all right?" he demanded.

"I think so," replied Don. "Tell us what happened to you."

"Later, later," replied the business manager. "First look after the bags."

More to satisfy the business manager's insistence than through any worry over the safety of the two bags which he planned to take to Professor Duer, Don went out to the car and examined the baggage compartment at the rear of the coupe.

His examination of the lock on the compartment brought the startling revelation that there had been a desperate attempt to open it. In haste Don inserted the key and opened the compartment. A glance satisfied him that the contents had not been disturbed but he made sure that the compartment was locked before he returned to the lobby.

"Somebody tried to jimmy the lock and get away with the bags," he told the business manager.

"I'll say somebody did," replied Hendricks. "A fellow was so busy doing it when I came out of the building that he failed to see or hear me until I was right behind him. I challenged him and he started to run but I made a tackle for him and we rolled into the street. That was the last I remember."

"Lucky you've got a tough head," observed Ed, "for he gave you a wallop with a club or blackjack that would have killed anybody but an advertising man."

"Well you can thank me for having saved your bags," said Hendricks, "and I'll be mightily disappointed if they don't have some valuable clues after this experience."

"Learning that we had the bags in the car and attempting to get them is pretty fast work," observed Don.

"Just who is that aimed at?" inquired Ed.

"Your esteemed friend, the mayor," replied the managing editor. "Someone big, powerful and unscrupulous is behind the scene manipulating the little drama and he fits into the picture nicely. He's the only man I know who could have us watched so closely that he'd know we have those bags in our possession."

"But try and pin anything on him," retorted Ed.

"I'll admit I can't right now," said Don, "but we've a whole week ahead of us and a good many things can happen in that time."

"There's been enough happening in the last two days to last me for a long time," said the business manager as he rubbed his head ruefully.

"We've got to go on to the union station," said Don, "but we'll be glad to leave you at home on our way down."

"Thanks," replied the business manager. "I'll accept your invitation this time."

They gave him a steadying arm as they walked to the coupe and several minutes later saw him to the door of his home.

"I may be a little bit foolish," said the business manager, "but I'm going to look in all the closets and under the bed before I go to sleep. If I don't I'll lie awake half the night waiting for someone to come along and hit me over the head."

"It isn't quite that bad," laughed Don. "Whoever hit you was after the bags and I'll soon have them in a safe place."

After leaving the business manager at his home, Don

sent the coupe through the deserted streets at a fast
pace for they had only a few minutes in which to reach
the station. Few stop lights in the heart of the city
were still flashing their warning and the after-theater
traffic had thinned out rapidly so they made good time
and swung under the large canopy at the station with
four minutes to spare.

"I'm not going in with you," Don told his police reporter. "These bags are too valuable to leave any
place. Here's wishing you good luck. Keep your eyes
open and let me know any developments."

"I will," promised Ed. "So long, and don't let anyone take a crack at your head."

Don was shifting gears and turning his coupe around
when a taxicab, running at a high rate of speed, skidded
to a stop at the main entrance of the big station. The
unusual speed of the cab attracted Don's attention and
he involuntarily let his own car idle along.

A single passenger hastened from the cab, handed the
driver a bill, and without waiting for change, hurried
into the station. The light was none too good and Don
caught only a glimpse of the man's face. There was
a livid scar on the right side just in front of the ear,
extending almost vertically for nearly two inches, and
Don knew that he would recognize the man where-
ever he saw him again.

The managing editor of the *Press* drove back across

town at a more leisurely pace and turned the coupe into the campus of the state university, which occupied a large amount of ground between the business and the residential section of the city. Lights on the campus were few and far between and Don drove carefully. After what had happened to the business manager he was resolved to take no unnecessary risks.

The dark bulk of the chemistry building loomed ahead and Don swung the coupe so that its lights played on the entrance. He stopped the car, shut off the engine and unlocked the luggage compartment. He took two handkerchiefs from his pockets, wrapped them around the handles of the suitcases and walked up to the main entrance. Several minutes after he had pressed the buzzer, lights flashed on and he could see Professor Duer coming down the stairs.

The door swung open and Don stepped inside the building.

"Good evening, good evening," said the noted crim-inologist. "Come right up to my laboratory. I want to hear all about this mysterious disappearance of my old friend."

Don followed the professor up the long flights of stairs and into the laboratory on the top floor. It was a great room, that rambled away into all kinds of nooks and cranies, shadowy and eerie in the low lights that burned over two tables at which the professor had been working. The walls were lined with shelves laden with various scientific equipment and huge retorts and beakers stood on separate tables at haphazard intervals. It was in this room that Professor Duer had solved many a baffling mystery and Don felt singularly honored for he knew only the professor's most intimate friends were allowed here.

"I shall continue my work," smiled the professor, "but go right on and tell me everything that's happened. If I don't appear to be listening, just remember that I am probably concentrating on some one thing you have told me. I'm really not as discourteous as I may appear at times."

The criminologist took the suitcases and placed them on a table. He was a large man, with shoulders as broad as those of a star fullback, which, indeed, he had been when with Robert Durian he had been a member of the championship team of the state university. But that was some thirty years before and now the broad shoulders were stooped from long years over his beloved test tubes and microscopes and the brown hair was liberally tinged with gray.

While Professor Duer worked over the traveling bag and the suitcase, dusting them with a powder which revealed every fingerprint, Don related the entire story of his uncle's disappearance, tracing it back to the first part of the week when the publisher of the *Press* had hurried away on the unknown mission from which he had never returned.

"Most interesting," said Professor Duer, who had not once interrupted Don's story. "And I might add," he continued, "most perplexing."

"It's baffling to us," admitted Don, "and unless we find Uncle Robert before a week from Saturday it looks like Mayor Krieg will take over the *Press* through his demand $100,000 note."

"Which," said Profesosr Duer quietly, "would be a calamity for Porter."

"No," he went on, so softly that Don thought he was talking to himself, "that must not happen."

"One of our reporters is on his way to Beldon to-night to learn all that he can from Mr. Huckins, who Uncle Robert visited there and we're having a thorough search made in the hills."

"That is useless," replied the criminologist. "Your uncle could not have been aboard the plane when it crashed. It must have landed after it left Beldon. I'd check up on that point."

"We will," promised Don, "but how about the attempt to murder the pilot? The doctor says the wound could not have been self-inflicted even if Pilot Bain had a motive for taking his own life. Someone must have been aboard the plane until a few minutes before it crashed."

"Isn't it possible that he might have been shot from another plane?" suggested Professor Duer.

"I hadn't thought of that," admitted Don, "but we'll make every effort to learn if another plane was flying in the Indian hills that afternoon."

The professor closely examined the luggage Don had brought and sighed wearily.

"So many people have handled this baggage," he said. "It is going to be difficult to get good prints but I'll do my best. As soon as I get anything satisfactory I'll send them to the bureau of identification in Washington."

"When can we expect an answer from them?"

"Probably Monday afternoon," replied Professor Duer. "I will let you know the moment I have any information. In the meantime, keep me posted on any developments."

Chapter VIII

DON MAKES A THREAT

Down town clocks were striking the solemn hour of two when Don left the laboratory of the famous criminologist. He drove slowly home through the now-deserted and quiet streets. His mind was unusually clear in a detached sort of way and he looked calmly at the problem which confronted him.

His uncle must be found before the following Saturday. Where and how had he disappeared? Where was he now?

Those questions, Don knew could not be answered until they had found George Huckins, and traced the mysterious Otto Bauer, the second man in the air express. But perhaps Carl Bain, the pilot who had been the victim of a murder attempt, would regain consciousness in time to help them. He must keep in close touch with the Hunt home in the Indian hills. Or possibly Jim Greer and his party would find some clue in the lonely hills.

There were many possibilities and Don felt that they were taking advantage of every one. The best thing for him now was to get some sleep.

He left the coupe parked in front of the apartment and was compelled to walk up the four flights of stairs to their own rooms when the automatic elevator refused to work, which it did every time it was really needed.

Harm and Steve had gone to bed but they had left a reading light on in the living room. Don got into his pajamas and went out to the sleeping porch as quietly as possible but before he reached his own bed he heard Steve whispering.

"Everything all right?" asked the city editor.

Don smiled to himself when he thought of how excited they would have been if they had known what had happened to the business manager at their own front door.

"Nothing to worry about," he replied, for he knew if he told them about the attack on Hendricks they would be up another hour discussing the mystery and they all were in need of sleep. He would tell them in the morning.

"Come on to bed," grumbled Harm, who had been partially aroused by the whispering and Don tumbled into bed and fell directly in a sound and dreamless sleep.

When he awoke next morning the sun was streaming through the east windows and from the angle he realized that it was much after his usual waking hour.

Steve and Harm had gone and Ed's bed had not been used. Don hastened through the living room and on into the bathroom where a cold shower dispelled every vestige of sleep. He hurried with his dressing for it was after ten o'clock and he usually reached the office before eight. Steve and Harm shouldn't have let him oversleep but he had to admit that the extra hours of rest had restored his strength and sharpened the alertness of his mind.

The coupe was still parked in front of the building when he descended and he drove to the restaurant where they usually ate breakfast together.

"A little late this morning," greeted the waiter who always served them. "Mr. Garwood and Mr. Nichols were here before eight."

"Yes, I'm running way behind schedule today," admitted Don, "and Mr. McGuire won't be here at all."

"So Mr. Garwood said," replied the waiter. "I'll have your breakfast at once. The usual order, I suppose."

"Yes," nodded Don, whose thoughts were far removed from the subject of selecting breakfast.

Sliced oranges, cereal, buttered toast and a glass of cold milk were set before him and he attacked the food with a zestful appetite.

When he reached the office Steve had the first mail edition well under way and Don turned to the pile of correspondence which had accumulated during his short absence.

"Why didn't you tell us what happened to Hendricks in front of the apartment last night?" asked Steve.

"I was too tired to talk another hour," confessed Don, "for it was after two o'clock when I reached home."

"He's got a bump the size of an egg on his head this morning," said Steve. "I've never had much love for business managers as a whole but Hendricks seems to be an exception. Imagine him just peeling off all that cash for Ed's expense money to Beldon."

"He realizes the *Press* is up against it unless we find Uncle Robert and is willing to spend money to save the paper," said Don.

"What have you got on the explosion in the gas plant for today?" he continued.

"Not much of a story," confessed Steve. "About all we can say is that the state labor department is considering an investigation but as I told you last night there's too much politics in the background for them to carry one through."

"I suppose so," conceded Don, "but when we find Uncle Robert we ought to have a story that we can start and finish ourselves."

Don went into the composing room to supervise the final makeup of the first mail edition. It was always a rush to make the first mail and this day was no exception. Some stories were too long, others were too short and some were late in coming off the Linotypes.

Jud Brown, the telegraph editor, with his eye-shade cocked at a ludicrous angle and his shirt sleeves rolled above his elbows, was standing at the bottom of page one, trying to help the makeup man get several important telegraph stories in. Steve was equally insistent that two local stories were most important. While they argued the clock ticked on relentlessly and Gene Johnson, the gray-haired foreman left his desk and came over to the makeup table.

"Better decide what you want to do," he warned them, "or you'll stick this edition and we'll miss the mails."

Missing the mails with an edition of the *Press* was almost as serious an offense as committing a major crime and Jud and Steve turned to Don.

"I've got two telegraph stories that must get in the first edition," explained the telegraph editor. "The front page is the only one open now."

"And I've got two local yarns that are just as important," added Steve.

Don knew there was justice in each one's claim but there was room now for less than a column of type and the front page couldn't be ripped apart and put together again in the five minutes remaining before the deadline.

The managing editor scanned the front page makeup with a practised eye. The two column picture in the middle of the page could be eliminated. It showed an accident which had occurred the preceding night; important but not essential for the first mail edition. They could use it later in the noon edition, the second mail and the city final.

"Pull out the cut," he told the makeup man and while that was being done he leaned over and shouted at Jud, who was hard of hearing.

"Cut your stories as much as possible," he told the telegraph editor.

Steve was already busy looking over the two local stories he wanted on the front page, eliminating every line that was non-essential. By the time the makeup man had jerked out the cut they had the stories pared down as much as possible.

The makeup man picked up the gleaming type in handsful and slapped it into the yawning space on the front page with a preciseness that comes only from long experience. He was a veteran at his work and the wrangling of the editors meant little to him. His job was to put the type in the pages and he chewed methodically on a large wad of gum, but despite his seeming slowness of movement, his fingers moved rapidly over the page, sticking leads in here and there to space the stories out and even up the page.

"One minute," said the foreman.

"Don't worry," replied Don, who was standing at

the foot of the page. "We'll make it all right."

"Yep," grunted the makeup man. "She's ready now."

The first mail edition was going to press on time and the members of the editorial staff returned to the news room.

"Jud makes me darned mad sometimes," said Steve, half to himself. "You'd think the only news that amounted to anything was telegraph. You can't run a successful newspaper without all kinds."

"And yet not five minutes ago I heard you protesting that we didn't need those telegraph stories on the front page," chuckled Don. "Now you say we need all kinds of news. Just a little bit inconsistent but if you didn't stand up and fight for your own news you'd be a mighty poor kind of a newspaperman."

Don's personal phone was ringing when he returned to his desk. Harm, who had taken over Ed's city hall and police station beat, was on the wire.

"Good news," said the star reporter. "I've just been thrown out of the mayor's office."

"What were you doing?" asked the managing editor.

"Snooping," chuckled Harm, "just plain every day snooping and I was caught in the act."

"And for what were you snooping?"

"Well, I was looking for the records of the last safety inspection made at the gas plant."

"But you'd find them in the city building inspector's office," said Don.

"Oh yes, sure," replied Harm. "At least in any average city. But this is not an average city. I'd already been at the inspector's office and they said the mayor had asked for the records yesterday. So I came on over here. No one was in the office and I saw the filing case standing there."

"And you just couldn't help taking a look?" suggested Don.

"Correct, Sherlock, correct," admitted Harm. "What's more I had a perfect right to look in that filing case. Those are public records, open to every citizen."

"What did you find?" asked Don.

"Enough for a story which will distress the mayor," replied Harm. "The records in that file showed that the city building inspector had not visited the gas plant for more than a year preceding the explosion and the notation on the record added that the suspension of the regular monthly inspection was at the order of Mayor Krieg."

"That's a real story," enthused Don. "Of course the mayor came in just then and booted you out."

"Don't get ahead of me," chuckled Harm. "The mayor did come in but just before he arrived I took the original record from the file and had my back to the case when he came in. However, he suspected I'd been up to no helpful work and out I went."

"Hop a taxi and get here as fast as you can," said Don. "We'll spread this story all over the front page of the noon edition and carry it there all the rest of the day."

"O. K.," said Harm, "but before I come in let me add that the mayor wants to see you in person."

"This morning?"

"I gathered that he wanted to talk with you right away, pronto, in a hurry or whatever other adjectives you have." Don turned to the city editor and told Steve about the story Harm was bringing in from the mayor's office.

"That ought to stir 'His Nibs' up a little," chuckled Steve, "and will I put it on page one."

He glanced toward Jud Brown, who was bent over his beloved telegraph desk.

"And here's one time," he added, "when Jud won't be able to argue that his news is more important."

"There might be a tornado, an earthquake or some other disaster," Don reminded him.

"I'll take my chances," grinned Steve. "Where are you going?" he asked as Don put on his coat and hat.

"Harm said the mayor wanted to see me," replied Don, "and I think it will do both of us good to have a heart to heart talk."

The managing editor went down the back stairs to the garage at the rear of the building where he signed an order for one of the paper's cars. The same coupé he had used on the eventful trip into the Indian hills was rolled down the runway and he started for the city hall. On the way a taxi sped by and Don caught a glimpse of Harm, hurrying to the office to write his big story.

When Don reached the mayor's office a policeman at the outer door stopped him. After several minutes wait, the managing editor was admitted to the inner office. The mayor was alone, seated behind a beautiful, hand-carved walnut desk in the center of the high-ceilinged, white walled room.

"You wanted to see me?" Don asked as he advanced toward the heavy-set puffy cheeked man who ruled the city government.

"I'll say I want to see you," was the gruff reply. "Did you see that policeman at the door?"

"Yes."

"Well, the next time one of your reporters comes snooping into this office he'll be arrested."

"What for?"

"What for!" exploded the mayor. "Why for taking records out of my office."

"The record wasn't very favorable to you, was it?" Don went on. "In fact, it showed that the city building inspector hadn't made any inspection at the gas plant for months before the explosion. Furthermore, the building inspector, apparently afraid that something like this explosion might happen, made the notation in the record that inspections had been dropped on your order."

"You'd never be able to prove that," countered the mayor.

"Perhaps not," agreed Don, "but in the meantime we'll make things pretty unpleasant for you."

"You'll have to move fast."

"Meaning what?"

"Meaning just this: That by next Saturday the *Porter Press* will go to me on your failure to take up that $100,000 note I happen to hold. After that there'll be only one paper, mine, the *Midwest News.*"

"If Uncle Robert returns before that time, you'll sing a different tune," promised Don.

"If he returns," mocked the mayor, who appeared to be enjoying himself immensely.

Don was thoroughly aroused by the mayor's sneers and he let his temper get the better of his judgment.

"Careful," he warned, "or you'll say something that will help me."

"How?"

"You might," replied Don, "you might say something about Otto Bauer and the Indian hills and then I might go right out and find my uncle."

The mayor's cheeks reddened and his lips tightened with the flush of anger.

"And you must realize that there'll be a charge of murder against the man who shot Pilot Bain," added Don.

"Get out of here and stay out," thundered the mayor.

"I'll go gladly," replied Don, "and thanks so much for the information. I think I can promise we'll have a surprise for you by next Saturday."

As he walked out of the mayor's office he had the satisfaction of knowing that he had left a sadly puzzled and somewhat alarmed man behind him.

Chapter IX

KIDNAPPED

Don was not altogether pleased with himself and the visit to the mayor's office for he had said more than he had intended. It had been foolish to mention anything about Otto Bauer, the mysterious second passenger on the plane, but he had noticed the mayor's reaction and he was more certain than ever that Marcus Krieg had a hand in his uncle's disappearance. Now he must concentrate every effort to make good his boast that he would have a surprise by next Saturday, namely, the discovery of what had happened to the publisher of the *Press*.

By the time Don had returned to the *Press* building, newsboys were on the street with the noon edition. He stopped in the press room for a copy and then hurried upstairs.

Steve and Harm had done a good job on the big story. It was clearly and concisely written and placed the lack of proper inspections in the gas plant squarely on the mayor. The engraving department had tried its best to get a facsimile of the record sheet Harm had obtained made in time for the edition but they had failed by five minutes. It would go in the second mail and the city final. The main thing had been to get the story on the street and into the hands of the thousands who were on the streets during the noon hour.

"Any news from Ed at Beldon?" Don asked the city editor.

"Not a thing," replied Steve.

"That's strange. He was to call as soon as he got in touch with Mr. Huckins," said Don. "Of course, he might be out of town and that would delay Ed in getting the information we need."

"Time to eat," said Harm, who had been writing and polishing up his story about the mayor for the later editions.

"I had a late breakfast," said Don. "I'll stay on at the office. Ed may call."

The city editor and the star reporter went out to lunch and Don and Jud Brown, the telegraph editor, were alone in the large news room. The rush of the next edition was nearly two hours away and the managing editor found time for a task for which he had little relish.

His uncle's disappearance and the mayor's subsequent action which threatened the very existence of the *Press* gave Don powers which he would not otherwise have exercised and he felt it necessary to make a thorough search of his uncle's office.

The room which the publisher of the *Press* called his

own was adjacent to the editorial office, but it was entered through a short hallway. The door was never locked and Don walked into the familiar room, a spacious chamber with two broad windows that opened onto the alley along one side of the *Press* building. Just outside the windows was one landing of the fire escape which led down from the floors above.

The large walnut desk which was his uncle's pride was in front of the windows, its top as well ordered as usual. The mail which had come during his absence was piled neatly in the mail basket and Don sat down in the large swivel chair and ran through the dozens of letters. The majority of the communications appeared to be of a strictly business nature and he soon sorted the mail into two piles. The smaller he reserved for further perusal. The mail sorted, he turned his attention to the various drawers in the desk. Only the fact that the *Press* and its staff were in a desperate situation enabled Don to pry into his uncle's office but he knew that his uncle would heartily approve and thoroughly understand. Perhaps some note, some letter might shed a ray of light on the mystery.

The desk failed to yield any papers which would help and Don went over to the letter file. For half an hour he skimmed through the carefully filed communications. Some of the material was surprising for it revealed how thorough his uncle had been in his efforts to bring lower light and gas rates for Porter, a crusade which had brought him the full enmity of the mayor.

There were letters in the file which would make excellent material for further stories against the mayor, letters which compared rates in other cities with those of Porter and which showed the unfairness of the mayor's whole régime. These letters Don selected and placed in a separate pile. He would turn them over to Harm and have him write a smashing series of stories attacking the mayor's pet utilities, a campaign which, if successful, would mean the saving of thousands of dollars every year to the residents of Porter.

When Don had finished at the letter pile he went back to the desk and picked up the handful of letters which he had sorted out from the recent mail for further perusal. He went through them again, narrowing them down to a half dozen which were either in a strange handwriting or unusual in some other way. Don went through each one of the half dozen carefully but they failed to yield any information. Several were requests for financial aid, and the others were criticisms of the paper which were directed at the publisher. All of them were carefully put back in the mail basket for Robert Durian liked to read all the criticisms himself of his paper and found many of them helpful in improving and strengthening the reader-appeal of his great newspaper.

The search of the office had failed to yield any information which would help and Don returned to the editorial office.

"Hello, there," called Steve. "We've been looking all around for you. Here's the reason Ed hasn't telephoned from Beldon."

The city editor thrust an Associated Press story into the managing editor's hands. Don read it at a glance.

A freight wreck had tied up all traffic on the Great Western line and the midnight mail on which Ed had been a passenger was held up a hundred miles outside Beldon.

"Ed will be storming all over that train," chuckled Steve.

"I know," nodded Don, "but that won't get him to Beldon and I wanted him to see George Huckins and find out why Uncle Robert was there."

"Ed realizes that," replied Steve, "and he'll get through as soon as possible."

"Let me know when anything else about the wreck or the resumption of train movement comes in," said Don as he walked to his desk. There he put in two long distance calls, one for Charlie Miller, the *Press's* correspondent at Akron and the other for the Hunt home in the Indian hills.

Five minutes later he was talking with the rotund, jolly editor of the *Akron Argus*.

"Sorry, Don," Charlie Miller said, "I haven't heard a thing that will help you out. Jim Greer and half a dozen of his friends are riding the hills day and night but they haven't discovered anything. We'll keep at it and let you know the minute we have any news."

Don thanked the correspondent and then turned to another phone where his call to the Hunt home was ready. Mrs. Hunt answered. The connection was none too good and Don had difficulty in hearing her so the operator at Akron repeated his questions and her answers.

No, Mrs. Hunt told him, Pilot Bain has not regained consciousness. How is he? Well, the nurses are none too optimistic now. He'd taken a turn for the worse but she thought he would recover. He was such a nice looking young man. Yes, if he said anything she would call him at once.

When Don finished talking with Mrs. Hunt he turned to find Steve at his elbow, another Associated Press story in his hand.

The managing editor picked up the story. Good news at last. Trains on the Great Western were moving and the midnight limited had reached Beldon only a few minutes before. They should hear from Ed at almost any minute. Perhaps he would have the news which would put them on the trail of the missing publisher.

The second mail edition deadline was two o'clock and as that hour neared the tension in the office increased. City reporters hurried in with their stories, rolled copypaper into typewriters and raced against the clock to get their stories on the city editor's desk ahead of the deadline. The telegraph editor bent a little more closely to his work for the second mail was the big mail edition of the day, its news going to thousands of readers outside the city.

Don's task was to supervise and co-ordinate all of the delicately tempered parts of the newspaper, to plan the front page make-up with the city and telegraph editors, to see that there was an even flow of copy to the composing room and above all, that the deadline was observed and the paper sent to press on time.

It was work which had become a part of his very life and he threw himself into the job with whole-hearted enthusiasm. When the edition went to press on time they all relaxed and looked at one another with a "well, we did it again" look and then started work on the city final which was to follow in little more than an hour. Great things can happen in that brief space of 60 minutes and a newspaper staff must be ready for the unexpected, capable of finding the unusual yet taking it in the usual way.

A phone jangled and Steve picked out one of the instruments from the three on his desk.

"Long distance from Beldon," he told Don. "It must be Ed for the operator wants to know if we'll pay for the call."

"Tell her we'll pay for it and give me that phone."

Steve repeated Don's message and then handed over the instrument. The managing editor could hear the Porter operator give the Beldon girl an O. K. Then he heard Ed's familiar voice but there was an excited, alarmed note in it.

"That you, Don?" asked the police reporter.

"Right," replied the managing editor. "What did George Huckins have to say about Uncle Robert's visit?"

"That's just it," wailed Ed. "He didn't have anything to say. I couldn't see him. He was kidnapped this morning!"

Chapter X

AN UNKNOWN CALLER

"Kidnapped?" echoed the managing editor as he grasped the full importance of Ed's message. He saw the only real, tangible clue on which they had based their hopes vanish and he grasped the telephone desperately as though that action might bring him closer to the reporter on the opposite side of the state.

The city editor had heard Don's exclamation and he leaned over the desk, his ear tuned to catch whatever further message Ed might have.

"A freight wreck delayed us six hours in getting into Beldon," explained Ed, "and as soon as I arrived I hopped a taxi and started for Huckins' home. The police and I arrived at the same time. Not half an hour before he had been called to the door and forced to accompany a man away from the house. His wife turned in the alarm and they're searching the city for some trace of the kidnapper."

"Got any kind of a description of him?" asked the managing editor.

"Meager," replied Ed. "Mrs. Huckins only caught a glimpse of him. He was medium height and heavy set. The only outstanding thing she noticed was a scar on one cheek."

Don's mind flashed back to an incident of the night before just after he had left Ed at the union station. The man with the scar! It was possible. Even then he might have been on his way to Beldon to kidnap George Huckins. But the train had been delayed. No matter. A man on such a mission would have found other means. He had probably hired a car and proceeded into the city.

"Was the scar on the right side of the face, about two inches long and livid?" Don asked Ed.

"Correct," replied the police reporter. "The Associated Press must have the story and his description on the wire if you know so much about it."

"They haven't had a thing as far as I know," replied Don, "but a man answering that description hurried into the union station just as I left you last night. He must be the man who kidnapped Huckins and he probably started for Beldon on the same train. When the freight wreck tied up traffic he hired a car some place and went on."

"Sounds plausible," admitted Ed. "I've talked with Mrs. Huckins and she said your uncle was here two days last week visiting with her husband. They were very secretive about their conversations and she hasn't much idea of what it was all about, except that it had to do with someone who was at one time a prisoner when her husband was warden. Then there was something about a sensational prison escape in which two guards were killed and the ringleader was never apprehended."

"How long ago did all this take place?"

"She thinks it must have been about thirty years ago, just before she married. Huckins, if you recall, was called the 'boy warden' and he started a lot of prison reforms that have been adopted all over the country. This prison break, so I gather, was staged at the start of his régime and it gave him a black eye since he was putting the honor system into the old bastile they called a prison here."

"Go out to the prison," instructed Don, "and look over the records of this jail break. If they refuse to let you have access to them, call me long distance and I think I can arrange it. Bring back every scrap of information you can and get back here as soon as possible. We'll decide then what's best to do in trying to trace Huckins."

"I'm starting now," said Ed as he hung up.

Don turned around to face Steve and the city editor saw the lines of worry etched more deeply in the managing editor's face.

"Another bad break?" he asked.

Don nodded.

"Whoever is engineering this little drama we're in is fiendishly clever," he said. "George Huckins, the only

man who could have told us Uncle Robert's mission
in Beldon was kidnapped half an hour before Ed
reached the house. But there is this thing certain.
Whatever Uncle Robert found out in Beldon directly
resulted in his own disappearance and in getting him
out of the way it was necessary to nearly kill the pilot
of the afternoon air express. Oh, if Bain could only
tell what took place after his plane left Beldon."

"Perhaps he will," offered Steve hopefully.

"It's too slim a chance to stake our hopes on," replied Don. "I talked with Mrs. Hunt up in the Indian
hills a few minutes ago and he hasn't shown any signs
of regaining consciousness and Charlie Miller at Akron
reports that Jim Greer and his searchers have failed to
find anything. No matter how we turn, we run into
a blank wall."

Harvey Hendricks, the business manager, came up
to inquire about the progress of events and Don told
the bad news.

"It's tough," said Hendricks, "for I've made every
effort to get additional financing but it all depends on
the return of your uncle before that note comes due a
week from to-day."

"We're not giving up yet," promised Don as his lips
set in a straight, determined line. "A whole lot can
happen in a week and we aren't overlooking a thing."

"I know you're not," replied the business manager,

"and don't hesitate to call on me for any assistance I can give."

"Thanks, Mr. Hendricks," said Don. "Your attitude is mighty helpful."

Disaster for a great newspaper may be only a week away yet the editions must go to press on time and the clock moved relentlessly ahead toward the deadline for the city final. The big news room teemed with activity, the final heavy rush of the day for the city edition had its main distribution in the city itself.

Don was forced to put thoughts of his uncle and the paper's fate into the background as he moved from one task to another, lending a hand at the telegraph desk, deciding with Steve on the importance of a local story, penciling out the libel in a court suit which a reporter, in his haste, had overlooked; then into the composing room to watch the final makeup as the pages moved to the press room. The surge and sweep of the press hour held the whole plant in its grip, the tension tightened, minds were sharper, hands moved more rapidly and even the clattering arms of the Linotypes seemed to move faster.

Then the final page was ready and Don walked about to the news room. One more edition, the green sheet with the finals on the afternoon sports event, and the day would be done. However, he was not needed for the green sheet since the bulk of the material which went into it was handled by the telegraph editor. He wanted to get away from the rush and nervousness of the office so he put on his hat and coat, informed Steve that he was going for a walk, and left the office.

Don turned away from the business district and sought the quiet of the state university campus. The rays of the westering sun were warm and cheery and the air of the September afternoon was a tonic to his tired nerves. His mind, which had hammered at first one problem and then another through the busy day, felt at rest and the cares of the office slipped away. He found a comfortable bench in a secluded clump of shrubbery and sat down to relax in the sunlight.

The problems of the hour seemed far away and he looked at them through clearer eyes. There was no click of electric printers bringing in the news of the state and world, no roar of the press, no chatter of voices or jangle of telephones to disturb him and the noises of the city were far, far in the background.

For half an hour Don enjoyed the quiet of his sanctuary, watching the sun sink toward the tops of the university buildings or a flock of birds, preparing for their southward journey, wheel through the sky.

"Good afternoon, Don," said a quiet voice which brought him back to the realities of the hour.

The managing editor turned quickly to face Professor Duer, the university's noted criminologist whom he had asked to study the baggage found in the wrecked plane for fingerprints.

"Don't get up," said Professor Duer. "This is my own favorite hideaway. I'll enjoy it with you and after while we'll have a little talk."

The September sunset, in all its glory, was upon them. The sunlight faded and a purple shroud descended. The western sky changed from a brilliant crimson to a rose which melted away into an azure blue. In the east the evening star proclaimed the coming of night and a few minutes later lights on the campus glowed. Day was done; night ruled.

Professor Duer pulled out a venerable pipe, tamped the bowl carefully and lighted the tobacco. To Don he offered a package of cigarettes.

"No thanks," replied the managing editor of the *Press*. "I don't use them."

"Don't tell me you're a newspaper man and don't use tobacco?" chuckled Professor Duer.

"They're not as rare as you might imagine," smiled Don. "For instance, I live with three others, the city editor, police reporter and our special assignment writer, and none of us smoke."

"How about drinking?"

"You can't drink and hold down a responsible job on a newspaper to-day," replied Don. "The tempo of the life is too fast. You've got to be keen, alert for everything .that comes along and drinking doesn't fit into that picture."

"I'm glad to hear that," replied Professor Duer. "When I was a youngster newspaper men had a poor name. They were looked at almost as a bunch of bums."

"All that's changed," explained Don. "More and more young men are coming to occupy responsible positions on the papers. Competition is keen and they demand men with ideas and energy. The big papers are encouraging young men who want to work for them to fit themselves especially for certain tasks so that they will be experts in writing one kind of news. Of course, that doesn't mean that they won't have to write all kinds of news. They will, but when the editor wants someone to write a story on astronomy he'll know just which member of his staff can do the job and do it well. If he wants a story about some new discovery in chemistry and its meaning he'll have someone else that is especially fitted for that; someone who has majored in chemistry, say, in college."

"No wonder the American newspaper is a daily miracle," laughed Professor Duer, "when you get an inside glimpse like this and learn how carefully men are selected for the jobs they hold."

"Getting out a daily paper is pretty much a science in itself," agreed Don.

"And speaking about science," continued Professor Duer, "reminds me that I got some excellent prints from one of those bags you left with me last night."

"Which one?" asked Don anxiously.

"The suitcase," replied the criminologist.

"That's the important one," exclaimed Don, "for it belonged to the mysterious passenger who boarded the plane at Beldon with Uncle Robert. I'll take steps at once to get a description of this man."

"Good idea," agreed the scientist. "In the meantime, I've sent those fingerprints to the federal bureau of identification at Washington and marked them urgent, which means we should have some word late Monday or early Tuesday."

Don told Professor Duer of the abduction of George Huckins just when they had pinned their hopes on information they had expected to obtain from him.

"The man with the scar is the key right now," agreed the eminent criminologist, "but of course you must realize that he is only the henchman of someone behind the scenes who is plotting this whole thing." ·

"I realize that," replied Don, "and Mayor Krieg fits into that picture very well. Uncle Robert disappears, the mayor obtains the note and calls for payment which he is aware is an impossible demand in view of the absence of the owner of the paper. If we fail to meet the note, he'll take charge of the paper which is worth far above the $100,000 which the note represents."

"If what you suspect is true the mayor is a much more capable and daring man than I've ever given him credit for being," replied Professor Duer.

"We've been pressing him hard for months," explained Don, "exposing the exhorbitant rates which his privately owned and controlled utilities have been charging, pointing out the slums which are due to his graft. The explosion in the gas plant the other day, due directly to an order from the mayor which stopped the regular safety inspections, was another hard blow. A man pressed hard will go a long ways, especially a crooked politician like the mayor."

"Of course," agreed Professor Duer, "but don't give up hope by any means. I wish that I could give my full time to helping you but I'm on a scientific mystery which demands my full time. However, if by next Thursday you don't have anything definite, let me know and I'll do everything in my power. In the meantime, find the man with the scar and you'll have your first big clue."

After leaving Professor Duer, Don felt greatly encouraged in the knowledge that the famous criminologist was ready to stand by and help if they needed him in the final emergency. On the way down town he stopped at a branch telegraph office and dispatched a message to the airport at Beldon, asking for complete information and description of the second passenger aboard the plane. Then he continued to the *Press* building.

The green sheet had been off the press for more than an hour and there was only one clerk, a want ad taker, in the business office. Don walked up to the editorial room where the chattering typewriters were now hooded and silent. There was only one light in the room, the shaded lamp where the city editor was working over his assignments for Monday.

Don came in so quietly that Steve was startled when he looked up to find the managing editor almost beside him.

"Whew!" he exclaimed. "You gave me the scare of my life. Next time fall over something so I'll know you're here. Where in the dickens have you been for the last couple of hours?"

"Sitting," replied Don.

"What?" asked Steve increduously, for it was hard to imagine the managing editor doing nothing.

"Just sitting," replied Don. "Sitting and thinking."

"Where and what?"

"I went over on the campus and found a quiet corner where I could be alone and think this tangle out. Professor Duer came along and after watching the sunset we had a visit."

"I don't blame you for 'just sitting' if it was with the

professor," said Steve. "Have you seen the *Midwest News'* final edition?"

"No," replied Don. "What's happened."

"Plenty," said Steve. "Take a look at that front page."

The city editor handed a copy of the final edition of their rival paper to the managing editor. In the middle of the front page was a two column headline that commanded instant attention.

"REPORTER FOR PRESS

ARRESTED; ACCUSED OF

STEALING CITY RECORD"

✳ ✳ ✳ ✳

The story went on to say that Harm Nichols, star reporter for the *Porter Press,* had been arrested that afternoon on a warrant sworn out by Mayor Krieg which charged him with the theft of records from the city files.

"Where is Harm now?" asked Don.

"The last time I saw him he was behind the bars in the city jail," chuckled Steve, "and just about as mad as anyone can be. Harvey Hendricks got the paper's lawyer and went down to get him out on bond. They ought to be here almost any time."

"Do you think the mayor will be able to make the charge against Harm stick?" asked Don.

"Hendricks doesn't think so," replied Steve. "It is only to embarrass us and discredit our story today which exposed the mayor as the man who had ordered that the safety inspections at the gas plant be stopped. It makes him look pretty bad after the explosion and death of those workmen."

"We'll make him look a whole lot worse before another week is over," promised Don. "Any news from Ed?"

"Telegram came an hour ago. He's got all the records you asked for, including pictures, and is on his way back now. He'll get in around ten o'clock for he took the late afternoon train."

Routine correspondence had accumulated on Don's desk and he busied himself with it while awaiting the return of his star reporter.

The telegraph office called with a message from the airport at Beldon giving a detailed description of the second passenger who had been aboard the ill-fated air express. There was no question now, Otto Bauer as he was listed in the passenger list of the ill-fated plane and the man with the scar were one and the same. The mystery was more clearly defined, centering now on the man with the scar.

Harm and the business manager came in shortly after eight o'clock with Harm still so mad he could hardly talk.

"Everything's all right," explained the business manager. "Harm has returned the original record and the mayor has agreed to drop the charge. However, we had photostatic copies of the original made in the presence of competent witnesses and the mayor will never be able to deny the story."

"And," added Harm, "the mayor apologized for accusing me of theft. I pointed out that I had a right to have access to those records."

"No wonder he apologized," laughed the business manager. "You're no lightweight, Harm, and I've never seen anyone madder than you were. The mayor was afraid you might lift one of those big hams you call hands and pop him."

"I'd have liked nothing better," agreed Harm, "but I've had enough jail for a while. Now let's eat. I got in jail too late for supper."

Don protested that he had too much to do but would Steve bring him a bottle of cold milk and several sandwiches? Steve would, so they departed, leaving Don alone in the shadowy news room.

He had been working not more than ten minutes when a sound, just what, he couldn't have said, disturbed him. The night noise of the city was ever in the background but this was sharper, something in the building; a sound as though someone was trying to open a window.

Don snapped off the light over his desk and waited for it to come again. A street car a block away clanged for an intersection but as that sound died away Don heard again the noise which had aroused his attention. It was muffled as though coming through a wall or door but there was no question but that someone was slowly, cautiously raising a window; someone was attempting to enter his uncle's office.

Chapter XI

THE MAN WITH THE SCAR

The realization that someone was attempting to enter his uncle's private office did not greatly alarm Don for by this time he had come to expect the unexpected. He remembered that Steve kept a flashlight in his desk and he felt his way over to the city editor's desk where he found the flashlight. It might come in handy in the dark if he succeeded in entering his uncle's office without alarming the intruder.

Don listened carefully and heard the sound of the window coming down. The invader was in the office. He was smart, at least, in lowering the window so that any casual passerby in the alley would not see it and turn in an alarm.

The managing editor moved slowly across the news room and slipped down the short hall that led to his uncle's office. Outside the door he waited for some sound from within. There was the noise of a drawer being opened cautiously and through the glass of the upper half of the door Don could see a fingerpoint of light. The intruder was going through his uncle's desk, examining the contents with the aid of a small flashlight.

Don turned the doorknob, opening it by the fraction

of the inch at a time. When the door was open three or four inches he could discern the shadowy outline of a man bent over the desk. The two large windows behind the desk let in just enough light from the alley to silhouette the man.

The managing editor was half way across the threshold when the door creaked. The finger of light which had been on the desk shot upward and struck him full in the face. He heard a startled exclamation and at the same time turned on the beam of his own flashlight, directing it toward the intruder. Don uttered an involuntary cry as his light fell on the features of the man. The visitor was the man with the scarred face!

Here, almost in the very heart of the *Press* building, was this man whom Don believed to be the key in the mystery, the man responsible for the abduction only that very morning of George Huckins in Beldon. Now he was in Porter, ransacking the office of the publisher of the *Press*. Don gathered himself for a fight. Whatever the odds, this man must be held and made to talk.

"Don't come any nearer," warned the man at the desk, his voice low but harsh, "and turn off that flashlight."

Don obeyed the first command but he kept the flashlight turned on the intruder.

"Turn off that flashlight!" the command snapped through the room a second time.

With surprising speed Don obeyed. The light
snapped out and his arm came back in a quick movement. With a startled cry the visitor saw what was
happening. Don turned the flashlight, the only available article, into a missle which went whistling through
the air.

One end of the heavy torch caught the marauder in
the forehead and he groaned and stumbled forward,
his own tiny flashlight falling to the floor where it lay
unnoticed.

Don leaped across the room and was almost on the
invader when the man with the scar lurched half erect
and the managing editor caught the gleam of a gun
in one hand.

The flash of flame stabbed through the darkness
and the bullet twitched the sleeve of his coat. It had
been close, far too close for comfort but before the
man with the scar could fire again, Don was on him,
grappling at close quarters for the gun.

Don was well developed physically and kept himself in good condition but he found the man on the
floor a worthy match and in the first seconds of their
struggle knew that he would be hard put to conquer
the unknown visitor.

The managing editor grabbed for the gun and they
rolled over and over on the floor, first one on top and
then the other. They crashed into the desk and the

man with the scar cried out in sudden pain. The gun skidded along the floor and the desperate fight was resumed.

Don gained a temporary advantage and banged his opponent's head against the floor with great gusto. He felt the grip of the man underneath weaken and resistance slump. Satisfied that the fight was over, he crawled away from his opponent and reached for the telephone on the desk. He'd call Steve and the others from the nearby restaurant where they always ate. He had hardly reached the telephone when he heard someone crawling behind him. The man with the scar had faked his submission. While Don had been hunting for the telephone, he had started a quiet search for the gun.

Don leaped in the direction of the sound and stumbled over the crouched form of his opponent. He went down with the other man on top. The scar-faced man abandoned whatever ethics he might have had and used every device he knew to beat the managing editor into submission. He clawed, kicked and bit and Don battled back grimly, using his fists at every opportunity. Some of the blows went home for he heard the other man grunt with pain several times.

Then the managing editor felt a sudden sickening feeling in the pit of his stomach, followed by an intense pain that racked his whole body and stretched him on the floor in agony. His opponent had given him "the knee," doubling up his knee and driving it with all his force into Don's stomach. The managing editor was temporarily out of the fight and the man with the scar retrieved his flashlight. No word had been said after the start of the conflict but now, between gasps for breath, the man with the scar spoke.

"That ought to teach you to mind your own business," he warned, "and if you keep on you'll get a whole lot worse than that. Next time I may not miss."

He found his gun and pocketed it while Don, still on the floor, continued to groan in realistic fashion. He had been badly jolted but not as severely as he led the other to believe.

Don knew that there was nothing of value in the office to the intruder and he played possum on the floor while the man with the scar rummaged through the desk and filing case along the wall. Don was playing for time. His strength was coming back rapidly and then Steve and the others might return at any minute. He would take almost any risk to insure the capture of this man with the scar.

The methodical search of the office continued but Don realized it was nearing an end. The desk and filing case had been gone over carefully and as he knew nothing had been found which could have had any value to the man with the scar.

"I could have saved you all this trouble," volunteered Don. "I went through the office this afternoon and couldn't find a thing."

His words electrified the searcher, who leaped across the room and shook the managing editor roughly. The flashlight blazed in Don's face and he knew that the man with the scar was watching him closely.

"What's that?" he demanded. Don repeated his statement, adding:

"There is nothing of value in the office. You're only wasting your time."

"I wonder if you're telling the truth," mused the man behind the flashlight.

"Of course," replied Don. "Now if you'll be equally truthful you'll tell me how you got off that afternoon air express before it crashed in the Indian hills Thursday." He heard the other draw his breath in sharply as though astonished at Don's question.

"What makes you think I was on the plane?"

"The description wired from the airport at Beldon tallies with your own."

"It could be a mistake."

"But it isn't." Don spoke the last words with a quiet finality.

The man behind the flashlight laughed harshly.

"You'll find," he promised, "that you're not as smart as you think you are."

A telephone ringing in the news room broke the silence which followed the last words and the man with the scar moved uneasily. He made a final tour of the office, flashing his light guardedly.

Don knew that he was about to leave the office and he steeled himself for the encounter he knew would be inevitable. The other man was strong and muscular but Don, strengthened by the knowledge that the man with the scar was the key to the mystery, felt that he was his equal.

The man with the scar turned toward the window and in that moment Don went into double-barreled action. His hands were on the rug which carpeted the office and with his feet braced, he gave it a sharp tug. The rug slid on the smooth surface. The nocturnal visitor threw up his arms in a vain effort to regain his balance and then crashed headlong to the floor. Don sprawled on top of him, clutching for the hand which was tugging at the gun pocket. The gun slipped away from them and they battled on the floor of the office in a silent, desperate fury, fists flailing away in the darkness, banging into chairs and the desk, toppling the filing case with a crash that echoed through the room and then rolling to the floor again.

Don was fighting a hard, scientific battle, aiming his blows at the other man's midrift, hoping that one of them would be a haymaker. They worked around toward the window and Don caught a silhouette of his opponent. He bored in close, both arms beating a tattoo against the other's body. He felt his opponent weakening and he hurled the last of his strength into the choppy, close-in blows that sapped the wind and melted the courage of any average fighter. But the man with the scar was far above average and he withstood Don's fierce attack with surprising courage.

The managing editor eased up and stepped back. The move was almost fatal for a right hook that must have started on the floor and came up all the way caught him on the right side of the chin and jarred his teeth so hard they ached. His head reeled for the moment but he shook the mist from his eyes and backed away, this time a trifle more cautiously.

"Better give up," Don advised. "You'll never get out of town and in another minute or two my friends will be here and your last chance will be gone."

"Talk is cheap," was the sharp reply.

"Then I won't waste it," replied Don. "I'm positive you know what happened to my uncle and where he is. In addition, there may be a murder charge against you for the shooting of Pilot Bain and another kidnapping charge for the abduction of George Huckins of Beldon."

"You've got a good imagination," came the reply and Don realized that the man with the scar was groping for the gun they had lost somewhere near the desk.

He went down on his hands and knees and reached out hopefully. With the gun in his possession he would be able to hold the man with the scar until his friends returned. If the other found the gun first it might be just too bad for him.

Cautiously Don explored the part of the room near him until a sharper noise took his attention to the window. There, silhouetted against the night sky, was the form of the man with the scar. He was poised, ready to hurl himself through the glass and out onto the landing of the fire escape just below the window.

Without stopping to straighten up, Don hurled himself across the room. The man with the scar heard him coming and turned to meet the attack. Don swung wildly with his right fist and caught the other on the side of the face but too late he saw that he had been tricked.

The man with the scar brought his foot up in a vicious kick. His heavy shoe caught Don just behind the right ear and the managing editor sank to the floor without a sound.

The man with the scar paused only long enough to retrieve his gun. Then he threw up the window, stepped out on the fire escape and disappeared in the night.

Chapter XII

PURSUIT

The city editor, the star reporter and the business manager spent more time over their evening meal than they had anticipated and it was well after nine o'clock when they left the restaurant. Steve carried a sack with two sandwiches for Don and a bottle of milk.

The business manager walked half a block with them to the first intersection.

"I'm going home instead of back to the office," he said. "See you in the morning."

Steve and Harm said goodnight to Hendricks and continued toward the *Press* building which loomed up toward the far end of the block they were then traversing. In this part of the city street lights were placed at every corner with one at the entrance of each alley. In theory it might have looked like a practical plan for the illumination of the lesser-used streets at night but in practice it left large areas which were in ominous darkness.

"Ed will be coming off the ten o'clock train in a few minutes," said Steve as they neared the alley which went past one side of the *Press* building.

"Here's hoping he has something definite that Don

can work on," replied Harm. "This blowing up of clues every time we think we have something good is getting my goat."

They walked on in silence and passed into the circle of light from the light at the entrance of the alley. Suddenly Harm grabbed Steve and jerked him back into the shadows.

"What's the idea?" the city editor started to ask, but Harm clapped a none too gentle hand over his mouth and pointed down the alley to the fire escape which ran past the office of the publisher of the *Press*.

A man was backing out of the window, intent on hurrying down the fire escape to the alley.

"What under the sun does that mean?" whispered Steve.

"We'll ask that question later," replied Harm. "Right now we're going to see what that fellow has to say for himself."

The two newspapermen slipped down the alley, keeping in the shadows as much as possible.

The man on the fire escape made no effort to conceal his haste, and ran down the iron steps. He reached the bottom and dropped to the pavement below while Steve and Harm were still at least 50 feet away.

"Halt!" cried Harm. "Don't move!"

The man turned toward them and Harm and Steve stopped involuntarily. The face they saw was that of a man at bay, a man who was cornered and desperate.

"He's got a gun," cried Steve as Harm started forward.

"Keep back," warned the man at the foot of the fire escape. "I don't want to hurt you but I'll shoot if necessary."

Then Harm made a startling discovery. The man turned so that the rays from the light at the head of the alley played on his face.

"It's the man with the scar!" he cried. "Come on, Steve, we've got to get him."

Harm leaped forward and the gun spat twice, the bullets smacking into the wall of the building on the other side of the alley.

Steve hurled the bottle of milk at the man with the scar, who saw the bottle coming and ducked, but not in time and the glass milk container smashed into his shoulder. He cried out in pain, and turned and ran down the alley.

Harm started after him with Steve at his heels. They pounded along together over the uneven paving in the alley.

"Don was in the office when we left," said Harm. "One of us must go back and see what's happened to him."

"You go," said Steve.

"Nope, you're elected," replied Harm. "I like tough

boys like this. Just let me get my hands on him and I'll twist him around my neck."

Steve realized that further argument with Harm would be useless and he gave up the chase, returning to the *Press* building to see if anything had happened to Don.

The man with the scar appeared remarkably athletic and Harm found himself hard put to keep up the pace. Out of the alley they went, into a better lighted street and Harm knew what his quarry was planning. They were heading for the railroad yards and once there the hunted man would be almost safe from pursuit.

As they passed each intersection Harm looked anxiously up and down the side streets for a policeman. Three, four, five blocks they pounded along the deserted street, a little more than two hundred feet separating the pursued and the pursuer.

Two more blocks and they would reach the maze of tracks with their long strings of freight cars. The yards meant safety for the man with the scar. He lengthened his stride for a block but Harm noticed that he appeared to be tiring rapidly. If the chase could only last three or four more blocks he would have him.

At the last intersection luck played with Harm. A policeman was half a block down the side street, strol-

ling along on his beat. Harm's cry caught his attention and he came on the run.

"Stop that man!" shouted the star reporter of the
Press. "He's wanted for burglary of the *Daily Press*
office."

The man with the scar was within a hundred feet
of the first string of freight cars when the policeman
took up the pursuit.

"Halt!" cried the officer. The command was ignored
and the blue-coated officer grabbed his gun and fired
at the fugitive.

The shot went wild and the man with the scar
escaped to the safety of the long lines of freight cars.

"What's it all about?" the policeman asked as they
reached the yards.

Harm explained in rapid-fire sentences and the officer
whistled, in amazement.

"No wonder you wanted to catch up with him," he
said. "Come on, we'll have a look through the yards.
Not much chance, but we may stumble on him. Here,
you'd better take my night stick and don't hesitate
to swing on him if you can."

"I won't," promised Harm as they separated, one
to go along each side of the first string of cars.

Lights gleamed from the big mastheads in the yards
but the lanes between the cars were in pitch darkness and Harm moved cautiously. Most of them were

merchandise cars, their doors closed and locked ready to be made up into outgoing trains. A few were empties and it was in these that the danger lurked. The man with the scar might be hidden in any one of them and they couldn't afford to overlook a single car. It was slow, tedious work but at last they came to the end of the string where they met to compare notes.

"Not a thing," said the policeman who mentioned that his name was Terrence Murphy.

"No luck either," reported Harm. "Well, maybe the second and third strings will prove better hunting."

Half way down the second string he thought he heard someone moving ahead of him and stopped to listen intently. Murphy, who heard Harm's footsteps stop, waited in the shadows on the other side of the car.

The noise came again, the soft crunching of a cautiously placed foot in the cinders.

Murphy flashed his bulls-eye along the ground and two car lengths ahead, Harm caught a glimpse of a shadow flitting between two cars.

"Come on, Murphy," he cried. "He's just ahead of us."

The big Irish policeman let out a like roar and plunged ahead through the night. Harm, on the other side of the string of cars, raced forward to where the man with the scar had disappeared.

Murphy was playing his light to and fro on the cars, flashing it between and under them.

"He's taken to the tops," cried Harm.

The reporter and the policeman raced up the nearest ladders and scrambled to their feet on top of the box cars.

"There he goes," yelled Murphy, pointing down the long line of cars.

A weaving figure was running down the lane of tops ahead of them and Harm and the policeman set out in pursuit. It was treacherous work, this running over the tops of box cars in the night, but they threw caution to the winds and raced ahead. Gradually they overtook their quarry, who appeared almost exhausted by his strenuous efforts.

"We'll get him," whooped Murphy, who enjoyed nothing better than an exciting chase.

Suddenly the scene changed. The man with the scar dropped to his knees and faced them. His gun spat flame and Murphy, in the lead, stumbled and fell headlong. He would have plunged over the edge of the car and fallen to the ground if Harm had not caught and held him.

"The dirty scoundrel," groaned Murphy. "Just let me get my hands on him."

"Are you hit bad?" asked Harm.

"No," grunted the policeman, "but he winged me in

the left leg. It's just enough to keep me out of the chase."

"He'll make his escape now," said Harm as he bent over the wounded officer.

"Not as long as my name's Murphy," said the policeman.

"Here," he said, thrusting his gun into Harm's hands, "take this and follow him. He's about exhausted."

"But I can't leave you," protested Harm. "You'll never be able to get to the ground alone."

"Don't worry about me," urged the policeman. "Listen, the yardmen heard the shot. Some of them are coming down this string of cars now. They'll take care of me and I'll phone your office. Go on."

Reluctant to leave the policeman, Harm resumed the chase. The man with the scar was nothing more than a flitting shadow dancing along the far end of the string of cars when Harm continued the hunt.

The heavy exhaust of a freight locomotive on the other side of the yard awakened the night and Harm saw the man with the scar swerve and leap from one string of freight cars to another. He was trying to reach the outgoing freight where he would have temporary safety.

Harm was at least five hundred feet behind the fugitive and if it had not been for the yard lights would have lost sight of him a half dozen times. As it was,

it was follow the trail. A string of coal cars opened
ahead and Harm fumed as he was forced to climb down
from the box cars, make his way along the string of
gondolas and then climb up on the box cars further
along the yards.

When he was again on the tops he scanned the yard
for a glimpse of the man he sought. The exhaust of
the freight was barking steadily as the train picked
up speed and Harm knew that his time was limited.
He must make an important decision at once. Should
he run the risk of hopping the moving train and keep
on the trail of the man with the scar or should he return to the office, get more help, and follow the freight
by car until its first stop where it could be searched?
The last plan was undoubtedly the sanest but Harm
was far from being in a sane mood and he threw caution to the winds. The man with the scar was their
key witness. To lose sight of him might bring disaster
to all of their hopes and plans and he instantly determined to stay on the trail.

The reporter scrambled down off the tops and ran
between the silent rows of cars until he came to the
end of the string. He was at the far end of the yard,
a mile above the station, and one lone, large arc cast
its rays over the tracks and switches. The freight engine had thundered over the last switch and was on
the main line of the Great Western, headed across

the state for Beldon, the next division point.

Harm saw a shadowy form emerge from a row of cars near the main line and the man with the scar dashed across the lighted area, reach for the ladder on one of the cars and swung onto the train. The reporter waited until the car on which the man he sought had taken refuge had disappeared. Using the shadows as much as possible he raced for the main line. The freight was picking up speed rapidly. To attempt to grab a ladder might hurl him under the train if he missed his grip.

Harm ran back a hundred feet and climbed a freight car on the track which paralleled the main line. The weaving tops of the freight slid past not more than four feet away. He gathered himself for the attempt, ran almost the length of his own car and then leaped across the intervening space. He lost his balance and sprawled on top of the car but his clutching hands fastened themselves on the runway and he held on. The freight whipped around a curve and he pulled himself into an upright position. The yard lights faded and the long train picked up speed for its cross-state run. Somewhere ahead was the man with the scar and Harm moved slowly forward, intent on finding his hiding place.

Chapter XIII

NEW CLUES

While Harm had continued the chase after the man with the scar, Steve had turned back toward the *Press* building, worried for fear some mishap had befallen the managing editor.

There were no lights in the big newspaper plant and that alone was not encouraging. The city editor hurried through the lobby on the main floor, switched on the lights in the stairway leading to the editorial office and raced up the stairs three at a time.

Steve snapped on the lights in the news room. There was no one there.

"Don!" he called.

There was no answer and he called again. Then, remembering that they had seen the man with the scar coming down the fire escape from the office of the publisher, Steve hastened down the hall. The half-light that filtered in from the alley gave him an intimation of what had happened the moment he entered the office. He turned on the lights and in their brilliant glow surveyed the wrecked interior of the office.

The rug was in a crumpled heap, papers were scattered in every corner and the filing case had been knocked over. Steve was startled by something that caught his attention just behind the desk and near the windows. It was a foot, protruding at a grotesque angle.

Steve leaped across the room and looked down at the unconscious form of the managing editor. He bent lower. Don was breathing regularly and mumbling to himself.

The city editor ran back to the water cooler in the main office and filled a paper cup with water. This he dashed in Don's face and a few seconds after the cold water struck him the managing editor opened his eyes and blinked at Steve.

His first move was to double his fist and swing a haymaker that Steve barely dodged.

"What's the idea?" protested the amazed Steve.

Don blinked hard and looked at him owlishly.

"The man with the scar," he muttered, half to himself and half to Steve. "Get the man with the scar."

"That's just what Harm is trying to do," replied Steve. "Come on, snap out of it and tell me what happened."

Don was still in a daze and Steve went back to the water cooler, obtained a second cup of water and threw it in the managing editor's face.

This brought order to Don's groggy senses and he recognized his city editor.

"Did I just swing at you?" he asked.

"And how!" replied Steve. "If I hadn't ducked you'd have laid me out cold."

"I must have thought the man with the scar was still in the room," said Don as he gingerly rubbed a lump which had appeared behind one ear. "Wow, what a kick that fellow gave me. How long have I been out?"

"Not over ten minutes," said Steve. "Harm and I saw this fellow coming down the fire escape when we came back with your lunch. He must have knocked you out not more than a minute before."

"Did you say Harm was still after him?" asked Don.

"He made me come back," explained Steve, "and he kept after this fellow. The last I saw of them they were pounding down Ferguson avenue, headed for the railroad yards. Now what happened to you?"

"I heard a noise that startled me," replied Don, "and I turned off the light in the news room and came down the hall. This chap with the scar was in here ransacking the office and we went to it. How that fellow can fight."

"And you might add, how he can run," grinned Steve.

"There's one consolation," said Don. "With Harm on the trail the man with the scar will find a regular human bulldog after him."

Steve had been examining the interior of the office

and he exclaimed over a strip of splintered paneling on one wall.

"That fellow must have used his gun in here!" he said.

"He did," replied Don. "I was just plain lucky not to get winged."

The managing editor got to his feet. His legs were still a little shaky but his head was clearing rapidly and he had the youth and vitality that soon restores strength.

Steve happened to glance at the managing editor's left hand.

"You've cut your hand!" he cried.

Don looked at his hand and shook his head.

"That's not blood," he replied.

Steve grasped the hand and examined it closely. He looked up astonished.

"It's grease paint!" he exclaimed.

"What?"

"It's grease paint," repeated the city editor. "Here, rub it with your other hand."

Don did as directed and a reddish smear appeared on his right hand.

"Now who in thunder," demanded Steve, "has been using grease paint?"

"There is only one explanation," replied Don slowly. "It's the man with the scar. Don't you see? It isn't a real scar at all; just one put on with grease paint. It makes him conspicuous, which is what he wants. Everyone will be hunting for the man with the scar. To throw off suspicion all he has to do is take a handkerchief or towel and wipe off the artificial scar. Devilishly clever, I'd say."

Steve was staring incredulously at the smear of grease paint.

"Then there is no man with the scar," he said slowly.

"Only when he wants to be the man with the scar," agreed Don.

"Another clue tumbling about our ears," mused the city editor, "but there is this chance. If Harm is able to keep on his trail, that man, scar or no scar, will have a hard time losing him."

"That's our one big hope now," conceded Don.

They heard someone running up the stairs from the main floor and walked out into the news room to greet the newcomer. It was Ed McGuire, who hastened in the room breathless.

"Boy, what a trip," he cried. Then, noticing the disarray of Don's clothes and the reddened spots on his face where he had received some stinging blows, he stopped short. "What's been going on here?"

Don explained in a few words as Ed dropped into a nearby chair. When he had finished, the police reporter whistled slowly.

"Well, I haven't been on the receiving end of all the excitement," he said.

"What did you find out in Beldon?" asked Don.

"Not a great deal," replied Ed. "I'm afraid the trip was pretty much of a dud. If the train hadn't been held up by that freight wreck, I'd have been there in time to talk with Huckins. As it is, I was half an hour too late."

"Hasn't Mrs. Huckins any idea why my uncle visited them?" asked Don.

"Very little," said Ed. "She did hear some mention of the sensational Corvin prison break about thirty years ago but that was all. After I talked with you I went out to the prison and dug into the records. That was one jail break that succeeded and three of the ringleaders never have been captured."

"But I don't see any connection between the Corvin prison break of thirty years ago and the disappearance of Don's uncle and then the abduction of the former warden."

"Only this," pointed out Don. "Isn't it just possible that George Huckins, warden at the time of this famous break, may have learned something which endangered the men who have never been re-captured. Perhaps he learned their present identities or he may have strongly suspected who they were. It would be quite natural for him to communicate with Uncle Robert, who has been a close friend for many years. If they were the only two in possession of this knowledge it is only logical that they would be put out of the way if the escaped convicts learned of their knowledge or even of their suspicions."

"Then perhaps our man with the scar is one of those involved in that prison break of so long ago," said Steve.

"It is entirely possible," conceded Don. "He's an athletic, vigorous type of fellow but he must be nearly fifty."

Ed delved into his traveling bag and produced a cardboard folder which contained a number of photographs and sheets of paper.

"Here are all the records on the Corvin break available," he explained as he spread the pictures on the city editor's desk. The photographs showed three young men, all in prison garb, posed for the usual prison photograph. There was nothing unusual about any of them and they did not appear to be criminal types, an observation which Steve noted aloud.

"That's one reason why it was impossible to trace them after the escape," said Ed. "They got into Beldon and simply lost themselves. Another thing, they weren't taking quite so many fingerprints in those days and there are no prints on this trio."

The three newspapermen studied the group. The

first one was Sam Corvin, acknowledged leader of the break. Second was Curt Boldt, the best looking of the three, and the third was Put Breese.

"And you say they never found any trace of them?" asked Steve.

"Nary a clue," replied Ed, "but George Huckins, who was warden at that time, almost lost his job. He was starting the honor system and they took advantage of him. He swore he'd never give up until he had found this trio and it begins to look like he might have been pretty close the day he disappeared."

"What do you mean by that?" demanded Don.

"Mrs. Huckins said her husband was greatly distressed over the news of your uncle's disappearance and he told her he thought he would go and see state officials about a matter he had been discussing with your uncle."

"Did Huckins think Uncle Robert was dead?"

"No," replied Ed. "At least Mrs. Huckins gave me that impression. She heard him say to himself, when he read the news, 'so they've got Bob. I'll be next for they know now'."

Don had been studying the photographs closely, centering attention on the one of Curt Boldt.

"Do you know," he said slowly, "I'm just about convinced that our man with the scar is none other than

Curt Boldt, who escaped from the Beldon prison thirty years ago."

"Why do you conclude that?" asked Steve.

"Partially a hunch; partially a distinct resemblance," replied Don. "I think I'd remember those eyes anywhere and those in the picture here look like the eyes of the man with the scar."

"You mean the 'man who had the scar'," corrected Steve.

Don smiled wearily.

"You're right. He's the 'man who had the scar' for by now it's gone and I'm afraid he is too."

"How about the other two in the pictures?" asked Ed.

"I haven't even the slightest hunch who they might be," smiled Don but Steve had the definite feeling that on that point the managing editor was concealing some of his innermost thoughts from them.

The telephone rang and Steve picked up an instrument on his desk.

"Yes, this is the *Press*," he said.

"What's that?" he asked as he leaned over the desk.

Steve listened intently and said, "Thanks a lot," as he hung up the receiver.

"The man with the scar just shot a policeman down in the railroad yards, an officer named Murphy. He was with Harm at the time. Murphy gave Harm his gun and Harm went on alone. Railroad men who heard the shot that brought Murphy down found the policeman. They haven't been able to locate Harm but a fast freight pulled out just after the shooting and the man with the scar and Harm are probably aboard."

"Who called?" asked Don.

"A railroad detective," replied Steve. "Murphy, the policeman, had promised Harm he'd let the office know. Murphy was just winged in the leg; nothing serious."

Don picked up a phone and put in a call for the office of the division superintendent of the Great Western.

"I'm going to see where we can stop that freight," he said. "We'll have it searched from one end to the other."

The call to the superintendent's office went through at once but from Don's remarks Steve and Ed knew that the results were anything but satisfactory.

"We're out of luck," Don told them when he was through. "The superintendent was willing enough to stop the freight but it is past the last night station this side of the Indian hills. The next night operator is at Marston on the far side of the hills. The train stops once in the hills, at Walford, for coal and water, but there's no night telegraph or telephone operator there. It's up to Harm to get the 'man with the scar'."

Chapter XIV

SECRET OF THE HILLS

While the long freight thundered through the countryside, Harm moved slowly forward over the tops of the swaying cars. Once, when the fireman threw open the door of the firebox to hurl in a fresh supply of fuel, the reporter thought he saw a shadowy form three or four car lengths ahead, but he could not be sure and he moved ahead cautiously.

Near the head end of the train there was a break in the long string of box cars where two tank cars and three coal gondolas had been set into the train. Without question the man with the scar had taken refuge on one of these cars.

Harm waited until the train was passing through a heavily timbered valley before he attempted to climb down from the box car and leap to the lurching platform at one end of the nearest tank car. When he jumped it was with the knowledge that the man he sought might be waiting for him, but he clenched his fists and made the leap. He sprawled on the little platform, regained his balance, and hung on.

The shock of the leap had forcibly removed most of Harm's breath and he rested and waited for his strength to return. From the speed of the train he

knew there would be few stops made that night and
there was little danger that the man with the scar
would attempt to get off between towns. There was
only ten cars between him and the engine and he felt
sure that he would be able to see his quarry if he attempted further flight.

Harm made himself as comfortable as possible and
pulled his coat close for the September night had a
biting chill and the speed of the train intensified his
discomfort. One consolation he found was in the
thought that the man ahead certainly was just as uncomfortable.

The fast freight lurched its way out of the timbered
valley and the moon struggled through the clouds.
They were speeding through a peaceful farm country
where few lights glowed for it was past the hour when
most farmers are up. Occasionally the train aroused
herds of horses who thundered away across the pas-
tures.

Harm realized that Don and Steve would be anxious
about him and he debated the best course to get a
message back to the office. There was no telling how
far he might have to follow the man with the scar
so he scribbled a note on a scrap of copy paper. The
dimness of the light and the motion of the train made
it an almost impossible task but he finally succeeded
in writing a few words.

He addressed the note to any employe of the Great
Western who might find it, asking them to telegraph
his message collect to the managing editor of the *Press*
at Porter. The note finished, he looked around for
something to wrap it around so he could throw it on
some station platform.

There was nothing on his end of the tank car that
would serve his purpose so he put the note in a pocket
and moved carefully ahead along the narrow runway.
Harm pushed on until he reached the end of the first
coal car where he found several lumps of coal which
would answer his needs. In returning to the end of
the tank car he was using for a shelter he decided to
go back along the other side of the train. He moved
with extreme care and just before he rounded the end
of the first car, stuck his head around to make sure
that he would not walk over someone.

He jerked back quickly. Coming along the runway
toward him was the man with the scar. Harm moved
rapidly, retreating along the other side of the train.
He returned to his shelter without being discovered,
thankful that he had not bumped into the man he
sought for a battle on the side of a swaying, lurching
tank car with the speeding wheels of a fast freight
beneath was the last thing he cared to think about.
There were only two tank cars on the train and undoubtedly the man with the scar had been on the other

side of the one on which Harm had taken refuge.

The freight had slowed perceptibly for a long grade and he looked ahead. A few lights gleamed along the right side of the track indicating some village. It was the chance he had been looking for and he wrapped his note around a small lump of coal.

When they swung around a curve and neared the station, Harm watched hopefully for some sign of a telegraph operator on duty but there was no sign of life at the station. When the freight rolled by he took careful aim and hurled the coal-weighted note. He couldn't be sure but he thought he heard the crash of the glass even above the noise of the train. He had tried to throw the note through the window of the agent's office, one way to insure its being read.

The contour of the country was changing. The level prairie gave way to more rolling country and Harm knew they were getting into the Indian hills. The moon had gone under the clouds and the night was heavy and dark. With the passing of midnight the chill in the air increased and Harm beat his arms against his body in an attempt to keep warm.

The train jerked sharply as the engineer opened the throttle for the steep grades ahead and the speed increased until the click of the wheels on the rail joints merged into a blur of sound. They wheeled around curves at a dizzying pace and several times Harm was forced to grab the hand irons to keep from being thrown from the train. Then the speed slackened as they struck the heavier grades and the roll of the train lessened.

They topped one long grade and eased down the other side. The exhaust of the engine was down to a low rumble and Harm knew that the engineer was drifting down grade. The train shuddered as a heavy reduction on the air line sent the brake shoes screaming against the wheels.

Harm took a firm grip on the hand irons and leaned out for a look ahead. The beam of the headlight cut a narrow swath through the night and half a mile down the grade he could see a water tank and coal chute. They had been out of the Porter yards for more than three hours and were stopping for coal and water.

The reporter welcomed the stop. It meant even greater vigilance to see that his quarry did not escape but he welcomed the opportunity to get down and stretch his legs without danger of losing his balance and being thrown from the train.

Fire streamed from the brake shoes as the air checked their speed and they ground to a jerky halt. Harm dropped down on the side away from the coal chute and water tank and stepped behind a pile of ties along the right-of-way.

The glow from the engine ahead was enough to reveal the passing of anyone in front of him and he watched closely. In less than a minute he saw the man with the scar drop down from the forward coal car and move away from the tracks.

Harm waited carefully. There was nothing on this side of the track except the open country and he fully expected that the man with the scar had got down to stretch his cramped body.

The engineer whistled a highball and the train clanked into motion but the man ahead made no effort to board it. The long freight rolled by and Harm saw the man he had been watching step across the track. He followed at a safe distance and soon found that there was a small village not more than a quarter of a mile back from the track. This, then, was the goal of the man with the scar.

There were no lights in the village and Harm wondered where the man he was trailing planned to take refuge. The answer was not long in coming. His quarry disappeared between two buildings and a moment later Harm heard the whirr of a starter, followed by the muffled exhaust of an automobile engine. He ran toward the spot where the man with the scar had disappeared only to see the tail light of a roadster vanish down an alley that opened on the main highway leading from the village.

Harm ran after the car in desperate haste but when he reached the main road the machine and its passenger had vanished into the hills which huddled around the village.

The main street was not more than two blocks long, most of the structures single story frame buildings of the 1880-1890 period and many of them had false fronts to make them look like two story buildings.

Harm, thoroughly disgusted with himself and the world in general, sat down on the sidewalk to think things over. This escape of the man with the scar was no mere coincidence for the machine had obviously been left there and Harm determined to learn all that he could while in the village.

The gleam of a flashlight showed down the street and a minute later the night watchman accosted Harm none too gently.

"What are you doing here?" demanded the guardian of the village peace.

Harm thought fast. He'd have to have a plausible story or he might spend the rest of the night and Sunday in the village jail.

"I'm a feature writer for the *Porter Press*," he explained, "and just got off the fast freight which stopped here. I've been assigned to write some stories about the fall scenery in this part of the state and thought this would be a fine place to start."

"Yep," replied the marshal, evidently satisfied with Harm's explanation. Then, noticing the wrinkled and dirty condition of Harm's clothes after his ride on the freight, asked suspiciously.

"Why are you coming in on a freight if you're a reporter for the Porter paper?"

Harm trusted to luck and made a guess.

"No trains stopping here Sunday," he said, "and this freight was the only thing I could get."

"Well, your story sounds all right," finally conceded the village officer.

"Isn't there any place open where I can get something to eat?" asked Harm who was still in mystery as to the identity of the town and afraid to ask the night watchman.

"Won't be a place open until morning," replied the officer.

"How about a hotel?"

"No hotel either, but I can fix you up a room."

This plan proved satisfactory and they walked down the street together, the watchman lighting the way with his flashlight.

The beam played on a sign and Harm was glad to learn that he was in the village of Walford, which he knew was in the western half of the Indian hills.

"I thought I heard a car starting just after the train pulled out?" said Harm.

"You did," replied the watchman. "It was Curt Barton. He's got a cabin over on Lake Okoboji where he spends a lot of time."

"Is he in the habit of coming in like this?" asked Harm.

"Yep. Kindda queer feller. We don't know a whole lot about him since the lake is 20 miles over in the hills. He's in business of some kind that takes him away a good deal."

"How long has he been around?"

"Three or four years, I guess. I'm not sure."

Harm elicited little further information from the watchman and went to the room provided for him where he was soon in a deep sleep. Early Sunday morning he was up, took breakfast at the one restaurant in Walford and made arrangements to rent a car from the garage.

Before leaving the village Harm went down to the railroad tracks. There was no regular station at Walford but the man who tended to the water tank and coal chute was a telegraph operator of sorts and he agreed to send a message to Don back in Porter.

"Believe I'm finally on a hot clue," wired Harm. "Am going into the hills and will wire you late tonight or tomorrow morning."

When that message was on the wire, Harm started his trip into the hills, headed for Lake Okoboji and the home of Curt Barton, the man with the scar.

The road out of the village was heavy from the last rain and two miles out Harm turned to the right, taking the winding trail that led to the lake. The garage man had given him minute directions and Harm had a road map of that section of the state. The trail was narrow but smooth, indicating that it carried a goodly amount of traffic, which, considering its isolation, was somewhat surprising to Harm. But he was to have a good many surprises before the end of the following 24 hours, the condition of the trail being among the more minor ones.

It was a gloriously clear September morning and if he had been on a less pressing mission, Harm would have enjoyed it to the utmost. An early frost had painted its magic colors on the hardwoods and the hills were shrouded with the soft haze that precedes Indian summer. Makeshift bridges crossed the hurrying streams but seldom did Harm see any sign of human habitation. Once or twice he glimpsed a farmhouse in the distance but the country was not conducive to farming and the few who attempted it were able to make only enough on which to subsist.

His car seemed to be laboring harder than before and the radiator started to boil violently as they toiled up a steep grade. It was enveloped in steam by the time they reached the crest and Harm was glad to find a small lake in the valley below. He coasted down grade and shut off the engine.

Evidently realizing the temperament of the car, the garage man had provided a bucket which appeared capable of holding water after a fashion. Harm walked over to the lake, filled the bucket and hastened back to the car lest he lose all the water out the leaky seams. Another trip was necessary and he returned to the shore of the lake. It was a beautiful little body of water, scintillating in the morning sun, and Harm stopped for a moment to enjoy the quiet beauty of the scene. His eyes roved over the background, the rolling hills with their covering of many-hued foliage and occasional pine that reared its head toward the sky like a solemn sentinel.

Harm was about to fill his bucket again when a glimpse of something white on the second hill beyond the lake caught his attention. It looked like a sheet caught in the branches of a tree and Harm decided to investigate.

The lake was not more than a quarter of a mile wide and he soon made his way around the near end and headed toward the hill on which he had seen the piece of cloth.

The underbrush was thick and he found his progress materially retarded after he left the lake shore but he toiled steadily onward. He caught another glimpse

of the white cloth through a small clearing and in five
more minutes he was making his way up the slope of
the second hill.

Another clearing opened before him and Harm
stopped in sheer astonishment. Then with a cry of
exultation, he ran across the clearing and started climbing a sturdy oak without regard for clothes or personal
danger. On the upper branches he found what he
had first believed to be a sheet. It was the remnant
of a parachute!

Chapter XV

IMPORTANT INFORMATION

Harm took a firmer grip on his precarious perch and attempted to reach the dangling piece of fabric. It was just beyond his clutching fingers and he was finally forced to abandon the attempt and descend.

The discovery of the remnant of the parachute threw an entirely different light on the disappearance of the publisher of the *Press* and Harm hurried back to the roadster to get his road map. He traced the route of the cross-state air express, found that it passed slightly to the north of Walford and almost directly over the spot on which he was now standing.

His chance discovery had cleared up one part of the mystery of Robert Durian's disappearance. There was no doubt in Harm's mind but that the publisher of the *Press* had been forced to put on a parachute and jump from the speeding express.

The reporter returned to the clearing where he had found the remnant of the parachute and made a thorough search. A little further back among the trees he found a patch of underbrush that had been trampled, indicating, possibly that the second and mys- terious passenger in the plane had descended here.

Harm again climbed the majestic oak and examined

the piece of fabric as closely as possible. It was evident that every attempt to get it down had been made and that in desperation as much as possible of it had been cut away. The small piece remaining had been just enough to attract Harm's attention and bring the solution of one of their most vexing problems.

The reporter made a careful search but the heavy rains which had swept the hills that afternoon the plane crashed had wiped out whatever footprints there might have been and at last he returned to his roadster and resumed the journey to Lake Obokoji.

The trail branched and Harm took the turn to the left, which, he observed, was much more used than the one leading to the right. At the end of another forty-five minutes of slow progress he topped a sharp grade and looked down on the entrancing beauty of Lake Okoboji, a long, narrow body of crystal blue water set between the hills.

.Rugged islands dotted its surface and the virgin timber clung close to its sides. Flocks of birds, preparing for their southward migration, wheeled along its shores.

There was an easy grade down to the lake valley and Harm shut off the engine and let the car coast down the slope. The condition of the road indicated that it was frequently used and the trees thinned away ahead and opened into a clearing along the lake shore.

The reporter decided to stop his car some distance from the clearing and continue afoot. A wisp of smoke from the chimney of the large cabin near the lake shore indicated that someone was about.

Harm decided that it would be best to assume his natural role of reporter if embarrassing questions were asked. He had brushed his clothes that morning, washed the cinders out of his hair, and was much more presentable than when he had tumbled off the freight train the night before at Walford.

The cabin faced the lake shore and Harm rounded the corner before he encountered anyone. Then he saw a man down on the beach, drawing a rowboat up on shore.

"Hello, there," cried Harm. "Fine morning, isn't it?"

The man at the boat straightened up suddenly and Harm felt a queer feeling along his spine. He was sure that he was looking into the face of the man with the scar only there wasn't any scar. He stared hard. There was no mistake. The man before him was the same height and build, there was the same carriage of the head. But, there was no scar.

Harm had to admit that he was sadly bewildered and he was afraid that he showed his amazement a little too openly.

"Sure it's a fine morning," agreed the man on the

beach, "but don't you know this is private property?"

"I didn't see any warning coming down the road," replied Harm.

"There aren't any signs up," admitted the man who should have had the scar, "but it's pretty generally understood that there is to be no trespassing on this property."

"You're Curt Barton, aren't you?" asked Harm.

"Yes," replied the other. "Who in the dickens are you?"

"I'm a reporter sent up into the hills to write feature stories about the beauty of this country in the fall," explained Harm. "Back at Walford they told me one of the most scenic places was Lake Okoboji and that's how I happened down here. There was no offense meant in coming on your property."

Barton appeared somewhat mollified at Harm's explanation of his visit and he climbed up the beach.

"As a matter of fact," he said, "I'd rather you wouldn't say anything about Lake Okoboji. It's a sort of hobby with me, this beautiful lake and its surroundings, and I'd hate to have hundreds of people coming in here and desecrating the place, setting the timber ablaze with their careless fires and pulling up all the wild flowers."

"I don't believe you'll have to worry about that," said Harm. "It's too difficult to get into this part of the hills."

While they were talking another man came to the door of the cabin but after a sharp examination of Harm, withdrew. The reporter noticed the incident and wondered how many more men might be on Barton's property.

"Great morning for a row on the lake," said Harm.

Barton appeared startled and glanced toward the boat.

"Oh yes, sure," he agreed. "Fine morning for a row." Then, as though remembering something, he asked:

"How long had you been here when I pulled up on shore?"

"Just arrived," said Harm truthfully and he caught the look of relief that flashed on Barton's face.

Harm would have liked to have said something about a man with a scar but concluded it would be better to remain silent on that point. They talked of general topics for several more minutes and then Harm turned to go.

"Sorry I intruded," he said, "and it's been a real pleasure to see the lake."

"Oh, that's all right," replied Barton, relieved that the reporter was going so soon. "We don't have much company and there are some undesirable characters in the hills."

Harm returned to his car and started the return trip to Walford, a bewildered young man.

The night before at Walford he had been sure that the man with the scar was Curt Barton. Now, he had met Barton, and there was no scar on his face. Yet Harm was almost positive that the man with the scar and Barton were one and the same. They corresponded in every respect in physical details with the one exception of the scar.

The reporter made slow progress on the return trip and when he reached the lake was forced to stop and refill the radiator of the car. At least he had made one important discovery. He had found out how Don's uncle had vanished from the plane before it crashed.

The wounding of the pilot puzzled him for a time and he consulted the map. The Hunt farm near where the plane had crashed and Walford were some thirty-five miles apart but it was possible, just possible, that the pilot had managed to carry on that far. The map showed an emergency landing field at Akron and Harm concluded that was what had happened. The second passenger aboard the plane had forced Don's uncle to put on a parachute, then gotten into one himself and just before they jumped, fired at the pilot in a murderous attempt to seal his lips forever.

The brightness of the September sky faded and a storm dropped down out of the hills with startling suddenness. Harm put up the top of the roadster but it afforded little protection from the driving rain and he was soon drenched. The engine refused to answer the starter and he knew that the ignition wires were wet. It would be hours before the car could be used and he decided to walk to Walford. He couldn't get any wetter.

Harm took the keys from the car and started down the narrow, muddy trail. The mud was soft and ankle deep but he plodded slowly on. The rain let up for a while and he thought the sun was going to come through the clouds but the sky darkened again and the rain resumed a steady downpour.

Two hours of steady plodding found Harm nearly exhausted and he took refuge under a clump of oaks. These afforded some protection from the rain but there was no escape from the cold that chilled him to the bone.

The afternoon wore on without a change in the weather and Harm, hungry and wet, continued his journey to Walford. Darkness found him still five or six miles from the village and completely fagged out.

A clearing along the road revealed an upland hay meadow of some farmer with a hay barn. It was a welcome sight to Harm, who tumbled into the warm, soft hay. To have left his wet clothes on all night would have spelled pneumonia but he was fortunate enough to find an old tarpaulin in the hay barn. He stripped off his wet clothing, hung it up on the beams, wrapped himself in a coarse canvas and burrowed into the hay. The canvas was rough but he was warm and soon asleep. He dropped into the deep slumber of one who is physically exhausted and did not awaken until the sun was well up over the hills.

Harm's clothes were still slightly damp but he could not delay longer. He must get to Walford and send word to Don of his discovery of the remnant of the parachute.

The air was clear and there was a distinct chill but the road was almost as muddy as it had been the night before. Harm was famished for it had been 24 hours since he had had anything to eat. Just before noon he walked into Walford looking much more like a tramp than a newspaperman. His first stop was at the restaurant where he bought a sandwich to ease the pangs of hunger. He put in an order for a hearty meal and then hurried down to the railroad where the man who served as agent and tender of the coal chute informed him that the next train for Porter was the four o'clock local.

Harm scrawled a message to Don. It read:

"Have discovered important information. Your uncle abducted from plane in parachute. Too dangerous to say more. Afraid news may leak. Meet me at office at eight tonight and I'll have full details."

The railroad man agreed to get the message on the wire at once and Harm turned to face Curt Barton, who had entered the office unobserved.

"You must have had a miserable trip back," said Barton. "I saw your car stalled back in the hills when I came in this morning."

"I did," replied Harm, who had taken a thorough dislike to this baffling individual. "I'm hungry, tired, wet, and muddy."

He stalked out of the office with the uncomfortable feeling that Barton was laughing at him and he would have been even more uncomfortable had he known that Barton was looking over the agent's shoulder and reading his message.

Chapter XVI

BEFORE THEIR EYES

Sunday was a quiet day in Porter, broken only by the reception of the two messages from Harm, one the note which he had thrown off the train and the other which he had sent after his arrival at Walford.

"There isn't much we can do until we get another report from Harm," said Don, "but I'm afraid he's going to be in for a surprise. Even if he catches up with the man he's trailing he'll find that the scar, the one real identifying mark, has vanished."

"Yes, I suppose so," agreed Steve. "Looks to me like we've been running into first one blind hole and then another."

"We have," admitted Don, "but the records Ed brought back from Beldon may help."

"How's that?" asked the police reporter.

"Well, for one thing we're fairly sure that the man who had the scar and Curt Boldt, who broke prison thirty years ago are one and the same man."

"You mean you feel sure about it," interposed Ed. "I've never seen this mysterious fellow with the grease paint scar."

"All right, have it that way," laughed Don. "I regard the records as important. It's a cinch that George

Huckins was close on the trail of these men and in some way Uncle Robert was linked to the whole thing, either through his friendship with Huckins or through the fact that he might have made the discovery as to who these escaped convicts are to-day."

"Do you mean that some of them may be right here living in Porter?" asked Steve.

"Just exactly," replied Don. "Thirty years is a long span of time and since those fellows had not been fingerprinted they have had a good chance to escape identification. Someone, either Uncle Robert or George Huckins, stumbled on their trail again and thereby placed themselves in great danger."

"But I thought you blamed the mayor for the disappearance of your uncle!" said Ed.

"There are two sides to it," explained Don. "I'll admit that at first I did blame the mayor and especially when he produced that $100,000 note and demanded payment of it or control of the paper. Now I'm swinging over to this new theory. It's possible that the disappearance of Uncle Robert was just a bit of luck for the mayor who saw in it an opportunity to profit at our expense."

"Sounds reasonable," admitted Steve, "but I still have my suspicions of the mayor. He's entirely too oily and fat to be above suspicion."

The prison records Ed had brought from Beldon

and all of the material which the *Press* staff had been using in its attack on Mayor Krieg had been brought to the apartment where they planned to work out stories for the next week. Steve and Ed applied themselves to this task while Don scribbled on editorials.

When evening came and there was no further word from Harm, Don become restless and threatened to start for Walford.

"Harm's all right," Steve reassured the managing editor. "You stay here and be ready to grab at anything new. Then, if we don't hear from Harm by tomorrow noon, we'll all go out to Walford and hunt for him."

Don agreed to that program and put in long distance calls for Akron and the Hunt farm. Charlie Miller reported nothing new from the search in the hills and Mrs. Hunt said that the wounded flyer was still unconscious.

"If Bain could only talk," said Don, half to himself, half to the others.

"If he could," agreed Steve, "we'd have the key to this mystery." They went out to dinner and while at the restaurant heard a fire truck clang by.

Ed started to leave the table but Don stopped him.

"It probably isn't anything important," he said. "You can pick up the story at the fire station in the morning."

Five minutes later another fire truck rushed by to be followed by a third.

"This is no bonfire," exclaimed Ed. "Let's go."

They paid their checks and hurried from the restaurant. The trucks had swung around a corner and they followed. The fire was evidently on their own street, possibly near their own apartment.

"It's a real one," said Ed as they pounded along the sidewalk. "Hear it; smell it?"

There was silent agreement on the part of Steve and Don who were devoting their energies to the sole task of reaching the scene of the fire.

They turned the corner and stopped involuntarily. The street ahead was choked with fire equipment and police were spreading fire lines to keep the rapidly gathering crowd back.

"It's our own apartment building!" gasped Steve.

"Come on!" cried Don. "All the records of our investigations into Mayor Krieg's affairs are in the apartment."

They followed him at a run, displayed their reporter's badges when halted at the police line, and reached the street directly in front of their own apartment. The south half of the structure appeared doomed but the north portion, in which they lived, was still untouched by the flames.

"I'm going after those records," said Don and before

Steve or Ed could stop him, the managing editor ran across the sidewalk, and disappeared in the smoke-filled lobby.

The heat inside was intense and Don stumbled into a fireman who was making his way out.

"Better get out of here," warned the fire fighter. "This is a scorcher."

Don ignored the warning and sprinted up the north stairway. He was gasping and breathless when he reached the fourth floor but he gained their own apartment in safety. It was the work of less than a minute to get together the records he wanted to save and wrap them in a heavy piece of paper.

When he opened the door which led to the hall, a fiery blast of heat swept into the room and Don slammed the door shut. Escape down the stairway was out of the question now. He hurried to the other side of the apartment where the windows looked out on the alley which ran alongside the building.

The fire escape connected with the windows in the next apartment but there was no way to reach it. Even if there had been, escape by that path was out of the question for tongues of flame were licking out the second story windows and curling around the fire escape. He was trapped in his own apartment!

When Don dashed into the burning building, Steve had attempted to follow but Ed had grabbed him and held him back.

"No use of the rest of us risking our lives in there," he said. "We'll be more help to Don staying outside. If he gets trapped we'll be in a position where we can help him."

They passed an anxious two minutes and when there was no sign of Don, Steve refused to remain inactive any longer.

"The fire's getting away from the firemen," he said. "Let's go around to the alley side of the building. Maybe Don is coming down the fire escape from the next apartment."

They hurried around to the broad, paved alley and were just in time to see the flames break through the second floor windows on that side.

"Whew! This is a scorcher!" cried Ed. "Don will never be able to get down that fire escape."

"There he is!" exclaimed Steve, who had anxiously been scanning the windows of their own apartment.

Don had opened one of the windows and was leaning far out. There was a package in his hands.

"He's got the records," said Steve. "Watch out! He's going to drop them."

The paper-wrapped bundle shot out and away from the danger of the fire on the second floor level and thudded against the concrete of the alley.

Steve picked it up and waved to Don but there was a terrible choky, dryness in his throat for he realized the danger of the managing editor's position.

Ed had found the fire chief, big Frank Hannigan, and brought him around to the alley.

"The managing editor of the *Press* is trapped on the fourth floor," cried Steve. "He can't get back down the stairway or down this fire escape in the alley."

"And we haven't the proper equipment to reach him," groaned the chief. "Honestly, boys, it's criminal the way the mayor milks our department. Our big ladder truck has been out of commission for a month and I haven't been able to get the money to have it repaired."

"How about a life net?" asked Ed.

"It would be his last jump," replied the chief. "The nets we have are all old and he'd drop right through them to the alley."

"Then you mean you haven't any way you can get him down?" demanded Steve.

"It looks that way, boys," admitted the chief. "That wall of fire on the second story means we can't use the little scaling ladders. I don't see what we can do."

While the fire chief made this discouraging statement, Steve hastily scanned the other buildings along the alley. Just opposite the building in which they made their home was a similar structure of practically the same height.

"Wait a minute," he cried. "Why can't we go up on the roof of the building on this side of the alley and then shove a ladder across to the windows of our own apartment?"

"The big ladder truck back at the central station is the only one that carries ladders long enough to reach," replied the chief. "I'll have to send a truck back after one of them."

"That will take too long," snapped Steve. "Hasn't your department even got a good piece of rope?"

"Plenty," replied the chief, nettled by Steve's sharp words.

"Then get it," snapped the city editor. "All you can get your hands on and swing a couple of nozzle men down this alley to hold the flames in check as long as possible."

"What are you going to do?" asked Ed.

"Get Don out of that apartment before he roasts," replied the city editor. "Come on!"

They met the chief, who had found a large coil of inch rope, at the head of the alley. Two nozzle men, with their helpers dragging lines of hose after them, were preparing to concentrate on the flames breaking out on the alley side of the doomed building.

The chief followed Steve and Ed without question for he saw a desperate determination in the face of the city editor of the *Press*.

Tenants in the building across the alley had fled to a place of safety and they raced up the stairs and made their way to the roof. The building they were on was a three story structure, which placed the roof line almost on a level with the windows of their apartment.

They could see Don, a water-soaked towel wrapped around his head, wave to them and Steve waved back.

The city editor handed Ed the bundle of records Don had dropped into the alley and took the rope the fire chief had brought.

With surprising dexterity he fashioned a lariat and gave it a trial whirl around his head.

"My gosh," exclaimed Ed, "I didn't know you could handle a rope."

"I'm no expert," replied Steve, "but a good many kids learn to handle a lariat. I was one of 'em and here's hoping I haven't forgotten everything I used to know."

The only light they had to work by was the red glare from the flames below, which, by the steady roar, were making rapid headway in the building across the alley.

Don could see what Steve intended to do and he made ready at the window to grasp the rope when it came hurtling across.

The city editor gave his loop several preliminary twirls and then sent it snaking toward Don. The first toss was short and Steve jerked it back in a hurry. There was not a second to lose and he made a second and third attempt. The third time Don got his hands on the rope but it slipped through his fingers.

"I've sent for the long ladders," the chief said. "Maybe they'll get here in time."

"And maybe they won't," replied Ed as Steve prepared for a fourth attempt.

The rope sailed clear and true this time and Don, reaching far out of the window, grasped the loop and pulled it into the room. Cupping his hands for a megaphone, Steve shouted instructions to the managing editor.

"We've doubled the rope," he called. "Keep on pulling until you have the double rope across the alley."

Don obeyed the instructions and a second later two one inch ropes connected the two buildings.

"Make your end fast to something that will hold your weight," commanded Steve. "Then swing out and come across the alley hand over hand."

"That's going to be a tremendous strain," said Ed. "Think Don will have the strength to make it?"

"He'll do his best," replied Steve, "and I think he'll make it all right."

From the pull on the rope they knew Don had secured it to some object in the apartment. The fire chief fastened their own end to a chimney and they saw Don crawl out of the window, place his hands on the double strand of rope, and swing out over the alley.

Steve and Ed gasped. The managing editor swung like a pendulum. He steadied himself and started the slow hand over hand journey across the alley. The rope was none too large and it burned his hands cruelly, but it was his one chance to escape the flames and he kept doggedly at his task.

Half way across Don stopped to rest, dangling nearly fifty feet above the alley. The firemen below were making a vain effort to beat back the flames on that side but even while Don rested red tongues of fire showed in the third floor windows of the building he had just left.

"Come on, Don, come on!" urged Steve. "Just a little more and you'll be with us."

Don nodded grimly and smiled through heat cracked lips. He swung his body a little forward and back to gain momentum and then moved forward rapidly, one hand moving ahead of the other. He was coming fast, so fast that if one hand slipped he would crash to the paving below.

Steve and the fire chief leaned over the edge of the roof, arms outstretched. There was a dull roar across the alley and Steve glanced up just in time to see a solid wall of fire burst into their own apartment.

"Just a little more," he urged Don, who was almost at the point of exhaustion.

The city editor made a futile lunge for Don but missed by inches. The fire chief, a six foot three Irishman, reached out and caught Don's right hand just as it slipped from the rope.

In another moment Don was on the roof. His hands were chafed red and raw by the rope, his features blackened by smoke and lips cracked from the heat but he was safe.

"Thanks a lot, Steve," he gasped. "Looked for a while like I was going to stay over there for keeps."

"You would have if we'd have depended on the fire department to get you out," put in Ed.

The fire chief started to reply but Steve explained that the big ladder truck had been out of order two months and the department was unable to get the order for the necessary repairs through the mayor's office.

"Will you sign an affidavit to that effect?" Don asked the burly fire chief.

"After the narrow escape tonight, I certainly will," replied Harrigan. "I'm a civil service man and the mayor can't kick me out of office. I'll come down in the morning and see you."

Ed handed the bundle of records to Don and they stood on the roof watching the flames devour their home. Half an hour later the roof dropped in with a crash and the wave of heat that rolled out was so intense that they had to retreat.

"You'd better see a doctor and have your hands dressed," Steve told Don.

"They are a little sore," admitted the managing editor, "but not that bad. We'll stop at a drug store and I'll get some good hand lotion to stop the smart-ing."

"Don't forget we'll have to find another place to stay," put in Ed.

"How about the Hotel Jefferson?" asked Don. "It's near the office and the rates are reasonable. We can get a large double room and stay there until we decide on permanent quarters."

"Suits me," said Steve and Ed agreed that the sug-gestion met with his approval.

Half an hour later, when they had obtained comfort-able quarters at the Jefferson and Don had eased the pain in his hands, they sat down to discuss the fire.

"Do you think it was deliberately set to cover up an attempt to get the records in our apartment?" asked Steve.

"No I don't," replied Don. "For one thing I couldn't find any evidence of anyone having been in the apart-ment. Now let's see if all the records are here."

They went through the bundle of papers they prized so highly but failed to find anything missing.

"I'm pretty well convinced that the fire was just an accident," said Don, "but we'll make an investigation in the morning."

A night of sound sleep refreshed them and Monday morning they were ready to face their problems with new vigor.

Ed was detailed to make an investigation of the fire while Steve and Don went to the office. The managing editor was disappointed when there was no further word from Harm but Steve prevailed upon him to at least wait until noon before he started for Walford.

The fire chief kept his word and by mid-forenoon they had an affidavit which would make things uncomfortable for the mayor.

"Put the story of the fire and the chief's affidavit on the main banner on page one," Don told Steve, "and let it go through all editions today."

Ed phoned a little later to say that there was little doubt but that the fire was accidental and probably due to defective wiring in the basement.

Another important message came during the morning, a telephone call from Professor Duer.

"I've some rather discouraging news," the criminologist told Don. "The report from the Washington bureau of identification is at hand and they have no record of any of the fingerprints we found on the luggage taken from the wrecked plane."

"That is disheartening," admitted Don, "for I had hoped that there might be some clue in the prints on that baggage."

"Are there any other developments?" asked the professor.

Don related in detail what had happened since he

had last talked with the professor and his suspicion
that the man with the scar was also Curt Boldt, one of
the trio who had fled from the state prison in the
famous Corvin break of thirty years ago.

"Not at all an improbable theory," affirmed Professor
Duer. "Keep after this fellow and I think you'll run
the mystery to earth. And remember, if you have nothing more definite than this by Thursday I'll drop everything and do whatever I can."

The news from the professor that the fingerprints
on the baggage found in the plane had failed to give
them any further clues was disturbing for Don had
placed substantial hope in that angle. It seemed that
every time they developed a new lead it faded into
nothingness and left them just where they had started—
confronted with the baffling mystery of his uncle's
disappearance. But if he thought the news from the
professor was to be the one discouraging event of the
morning he was mistaken. Just before noon there was
a long distance call from the Hunt farm in the Indian
hills.

Bain, the pilot of the air express, was dying.

The lips of the one man who could have told them
exactly what had taken place that eventful Thursday
afternoon were to be sealed forever.

A mist swam before Don's eyes and he sat like a man
in a trance, neither moving nor thinking until Steve

came over to ask him a question about the noon edition.

"Do you want any changes in the front page?" the city editor wanted to know.

Don glanced dully at the clock. There was just time to get a bulletin on the front page of the noon edition. The urge of the press hour was in the room and Don's trained mind and body responded.

"Yes," he replied. "A call from the Hunt farm says Carl Bain is dying. I'll write a hundred word bulletin. Tear out a place for it in column seven. I'll have it ready at once."

Steve hurried away to warn the foreman of the composing room of the change on the front page and Don turned to his typewriter, where, with flying fingers, he wrote the bulletin about the flyer. Two minutes later the copy was on its way to the composing room and the noon-day crowds in the street would soon know that a gallant airman was on his final flight.

The solution of the whole mystery now depended on Harm, who had trailed Otto Bauer, second passenger on the plane and the man with the scar, into the Indian hills. Don fumed at his own inactivity but Steve counseled that the wise thing to do was await further word from Harm and the managing editor was forced to agree that such a plan appeared best.

"But," Don assured Steve, "if we don't hear by nightfall at the latest, I'm going to Walford and start hunting for Harm. Something might have happened to him."

When they returned to the office after lunch a telegram was on Don's desk. The message was from Harm. Good news at last. Things were breaking their way. Harm had made important discoveries in the Indian hills, he had learned how Don's uncle had been abducted, and would meet them at the office at eight that night.

At two that afternoon there was another call from the Hunt farm. Carl Bain was dead.

Don was prepared for that news and its final coming was not as much of a shock as though it had come without warning but he was visibly shaken by the airman's death. There was little question of the desperateness of the men who had made away with his uncle for he was convinced that no one man could have done the job alone. There must have been an accomplice somewhere on the ground.

Don himself wrote the story of the tragic death of the air express pilot and the aviation company authorized a reward of $5,000 for the capture of the man or men who had been responsible for his murder. Those stories, plus the one of the fire and the new attack on Mayor Krieg through the fire chief, made the front page of the city final alive with startling headlines.

When the last edition for the day was off the press, Don, Steve and Ed gathered around the managing editor's desk for a conference.

"The best thing we can do is go home and get some rest," advised Steve. "Harm's telegram said that he was coming back with important news, which, if I know Harm, means we're going to be in for some busy hours."

Don finally agreed to the city editor's suggestion and they went to their new quarters in the Hotel Jefferson to rest for an hour and a half. After dinner they returned to the office to await the arrival of Harm.

The managing editor got out the records Ed had brought from the state prison at Beldon and studied the faces of the three men who had staged the daring break thirty years before. The more he studied them the more convinced he became that the man with the scar and Curt Boldt were one and the same, the man who had put his name in the passenger list of the air express as Otto Bauer and who had been directly responsible for his uncle's disappearance. The picture of Sam Corvin also aroused an uneasy feeling, a reaction that he knew this man who had led the break. It was a feeling that Don couldn't define and he finally put it down to a sharpened suspicion and shelved the thought. Put Breese, the third member of the trio, appeared to be a weakling who had probably followed in the footsteps of the others.

Reviewing the whole trend of events, Don became more convinced than ever that the prison break of years ago and his uncle's disappearance followed by the abduction of George Huckins, the former warden, were all closely woven together. If he could only put his finger on the key thread he could untangle the situation in a hurry and perhaps Harm, who even then was hurrying toward the office, held this key.

Steve was working at his desk but Ed paced impatiently up and down in front of the windows which looked down on the street.

"Harm ought to be here any minute," he said, looking at the clock. It was eight-fifteen.

"Probably delayed a few minutes," said Steve, "especially if he came in on a Great Western local."

Ed called the union station and learned that the local from the west had just pulled in, twenty minutes late.

"He'll be here in a few minutes," he announced as he resumed his vigil at the windows.

A small coupe rolled down the street and turned into the alley alongside the *Press* building. Ed attached little importance to this but he would have been greatly alarmed had he seen the driver stop the machine and leave it parked near the side entrance with the motor running. Several minutes later a taxicab slowed down at the main entrance of the building and Ed saw Harm get out and pay the driver.

The taxi lurched away and Harm hurried into the main lobby of the *Press* building.

"Harm's on his way up now," Ed called. "He just got out of a taxi."

The trio in the office waited expectantly for the reporter to hurry up the stairs and rush in. Instead, they heard a sharp cry, followed by the report of a pistol shot.

"Come on," cried Don, "Harm's in trouble."

They raced down the stairs and into the darkened lobby. Steve snapped on the lights but there was no sign of Harm. He had disappeared almost before their eyes. From the alley came the sound of the clashing gears of an automobile and they ran out just in time to see the black coupe speed down the alley and vanish into the next street.

Chapter XVII

THE WARNING LETTER

"Well, what do you make of that?" asked Ed as they stared after the coupe.

"Just this," replied Don, "Harm learned too much while he was in the Indian hills near Walford. They had to get him out of the way but they didn't catch up with him until he reached Porter."

"I'm going to get busy on the phone and see if the police will do anything for us," said Ed and he hurried up to the editorial office where he turned in an alarm and asked that all roads out of the city be watched for the black coupe.

"That car will be miles away from here before the police are out," said Don bitterly. "They'll go out and take a look but they won't hurt themselves since it is the *Press* asking for help."

"I suppose you're right," agreed Ed.

Steve was busy looking around the lobby for some indication that Harm might have been injured by the shot they heard. He found no sign that the reporter might have been wounded and they dug the bullet out of a crack between the marble baseboard where it had lodged.

"I'm going to save this as a souvenir," said Ed as he pocketed the misshapen leaden slug.

"And I'm going into the Indian hills," said Don. "There's one thing for which we can thank Harm. His message from Walford gave us a real clue on where to start from and when we find Harm we'll find Uncle Robert and George Huckins."

Don communicated the latest events to the business manager and made arrangements to be away from the office for several days. Steve would remain in charge of the paper and Ed would accompany Don on the trip into the hills.

They visited an all-night clothes shop where they obtained heavy jackets for the September evenings in the hills would be raw and cold.

The business manager came down, opened the safe and supplied Don with a goodly amount of expense money.

"This is getting about the limit," he declared, "when they come into our own building and kidnap our reporters."

"It's gone the limit," said Don, "for now we know where to start and unless I miss my guess Harm will have left some kind of a trail for us to follow. This is Monday night and I'll promise you that before that $100,000 note is due Saturday, Uncle Robert will be back in what's left of his office."

"If he isn't the *Press* will fall under the control of Mayor Krieg," replied the business manager, "so do your best."

Don took the same coupe he had used on his first trip to the Indian hills and shortly before midnight they sped out of Porter, bound on a quest which was to hold undreamed of surprises and thrills for both Don and Ed.

They followed the cross-state paved road for the first fifty miles and then swung off to the left on the dirt road that led to Walford. The road was in miserable condition, crooked and so deeply rutted that it was necessary for them to keep the car in second gear most of the time. They crawled along at ten and twelve miles an hour for mile after mile. Occasionally they would strike three or four miles where some enterprising farmers had dragged the road but these were few and far between.

Don and Ed alternated at the wheel but sleep was impossible for the one who was not driving and they complained bitterly of the condition of the road.

They were still some miles from Walford when the sky in the east reddened. The sun, a disk of fire, peeped over the hills and its rays soon melted the frost crystals in the valleys. It was seven o'clock when they turned on to a better road and found a sign that read: "Walford, five miles."

"The end of the long, long trail," groaned Ed as he yawned and stretched his legs.

"You're wrong," replied Don with little sympathy.

"This is only the beginning of what may be a long, long trail."

"Then let's hope that we're over the worst of the bumps," said Ed. "I've had about all I can stand for the current season."

When they reached Walford, Don stopped the coupe at the town's one garage to have the gasoline and oil replenished and to make inquiry about Harm.

The garage man proved talkative.

"Sure, I know him," he said. "Good looking, heavy-built sort of a fellow. Said he was a reporter up here to write stories about the hills. He rented a car from me Sunday morning to go out to Lake Okoboji. Got caught in a storm that afternoon and stalled the car in the mud. He started to walk in to town but got all worn out and slept in a hay barn that night and came on in yesterday. Left on the local for Porter and I've got to go out and get my car. Guess it won't run away."

"We're newspaper men, too," explained Don, "doing the same kind of stories. That's why we wanted to know what part of the country he visited. Anyone else in town know anything about him?"

"He stayed part of Sunday night over at the night watchman's rooming house," said the garage man. "He ought to be able to help you out but he's probably in bed by this time."

They paid their bill at the garage and went to the watchman's home. After some argument, they got the watchman's wife to awaken her husband, who came down to talk with them.

"Do you fellows happen to be from the *Porter Press?*" asked the watchman.

"Yes," replied Don.

"Is one of you Don Durian?"

"I am," said Don.

"Then I've got a letter that the other reporter left for you," explained the town official and he went in the house and returned with a sealed envelope.

Don and Ed read it together. Harm had written:

"Dear Don:

"I've just wired you that I will return to the office tonight but to play safe I'm leaving this letter with the night watchman. I followed the man with the scar to Walford where he had a car waiting and got away from me. He is known here as Curt Barton, appears well to do in spite of doing nothing and owns a large amount of land and a big cabin on the shore of Lake Okoboji, about 20 miles out in the hills. I rented a car Sunday morning and started for the lake. About two thirds of the way there the car ran out of water and I stopped beside a small lake to refill the radiator. A flash of something white in a big tree beyond the lake caught my attention and I went over and shinned up the tree. The cloth was a remnant of a parachute. The chute must have caught in the tree. Every effort had been made to destroy all the evidence but they couldn't reach this piece so they cut away as much as possible and trusted to luck no one would see it. Further back I found a trampled down place where a second chute must have landed, which explains how your uncle disappeared from the plane. You'll note that the air express line passes over here. Bain was shot just before your uncle was forced to jump and he attempted to take the plane on to the emergency landing field near Akron."

"My gosh," exclaimed Ed. "It's simple when you read it."

"Simple," admitted Don, "yet fiendishly clever in its simplicity." He read on:

"I went on to the lake and met Barton at the lake shore. He was just in from a row and appeared disturbed that I had arrived at that moment. Here was where I got the real surprise. Barton is the same build as the man I followed but he does not have a scar."

"I'll bet that puzzled old Harm," chuckled Don. "However, we won't be fooled by that for we know the scar was put on with grease paint and clever makeup."

Harm's letter continued:

"There was another smaller fellow at the cabin but I only got a glimpse of him and Barton gave me to understand that outsiders were not welcome. On the return trip I had a lot of bad luck. It started to rain and the car stalled. I walked back to town but was all in when half way here and had to spend the rest of the night in a hay barn. I had just finished sending my telegram to you when Barton came in the railroad office here. In case anything should happen to me, I'm leaving this letter with the night watchman who will see that it gets to you. Watch Barton!"

Chapter XVIII

THE CABIN'S SECRET

Harm's final words, a warning to watch Barton, would not go unheeded for Don and Ed realized that they were about to come to grips with a most formidable foe, a man they variously knew as Otto Bauer, second passenger on the plane, and, as Don believed, Curt Boldt, escaped convict.

The managing editor of the *Press* inquired explicit directions on how to reach Lake Okoboji and in doing so received another valuable bit of information from the night watchman.

"If you'd have been along about three hours ago you wouldn't have had to go clear out to the lake to see Barton," he said.

"You mean Barton was here earlier this morning?" asked Don.

"He drove in somewhere between four and five o'clock," replied the night watchman.

"Anyone with him?" asked Ed anxiously.

"I didn't see who was in the car," said the watchman, "but I heard him go through town and take the road to the lake."

Don glanced significantly at Ed. They were on a warm trail at last and they intended to waste no further time in following it up. After thanking the town watchman they returned to their car and, stopping only long enough to have a lunch put up for them at the restaurant, started out the lake road. It was in poor condition and they made even slower time than they had on the trip in to Walford. When they finally reached the lake Harm had mentioned in his letter they stopped their car and got out to find the piece of parachute cloth he had mentioned.

Ed sighted it first on the second hill beyond the lake and they made their way to the little clearing.

"My hands are still sore from that rope," said Don. "You'd better shin up the tree and see if you can get hold of the scrap of cloth."

Ed ascended the tree with little difficulty and even though he was lighter than Harm and could go further out on the limb he had no better luck in reaching the piece of cloth.

"We'll not waste any more time here," Don decided and Ed slid down out of the tree.

They resumed the tedious journey toward Lake Okoboji and it was another hour before Don saw a newly placed sign that brought them to a halt. It was placed at the side of the road where a driver could not miss it and read:

. "WARNING: *No tresspassing on this property. To do so may endanger your life. This means you.*"

Ed got out and examined the sign.

"Brand new," he commented. "Must have been put up within the last day or two."

"Probably was placed there as a result of Harm's visit," said Don. "Well, we won't run any risks if we can help it."

"What are you going to do?" asked Ed.

"Go back to Walford," replied Don in a loud voice. "I've had all the scenery I want and all the rough roads. Let's go."

Ed started to protest but he caught Don's wink and climbed in without further words. They went back down the road for at least a mile and when they came to a strip of grass along the side that looked as though it would bear the weight of the car without rutting deeply, Don drove the machine off the road and behind a thick clump of sumac where it was concealed from any but the closest observer.

"Now let's have an explanation of all this Sherlock Holmes stuff," said Ed.

"I saw someone moving in the underbrush along the road when we stopped beside the sign," explained Don, "and it would have been foolish to have kept on. We'll leave the car here and walk back."

Ed agreed that it was a good plan and they resumed their journey. However, they kept several hundred feet back from the road, a precaution which materially

slowed their progress but insured them from detection.
When they finally reached the lake they were a quarter
of a mile below the clearing where Barton's cabin was
located.

In spite of the seriousness of their mission they
paused a minute to admire the beauty of Lake Okoboji,
its waters sparkling as a September breeze ruffled the
surface of the lake.

"Queer rock formations here," commented Ed.
"Notice the large amount of limestone. And say, those
islands are practically all of limestone."

"Now you're remembering your high school ge-
ology," laughed Don. "This section of the hills is
practically all underlaid with limestone, which crops
out prominently here. There are some strange geo-
logical formations in this part of the state."

They moved inland from the shore of the lake and
made their way toward the clearing. At some distance
from the cabin they found a little knoll, covered with
underbrush, which afforded a hiding place.

"We'll stay here," said Don, "where we can see everything that goes on in the clearing without being seen
ourselves."

Ed made an important discovery when he sighted a
black coupé in the garage on the far side of the clearing.

"That's the car used to abduct Harm!" exclaimed
Don.

"The rowboat he mentioned in his letter is still on the beach," added Ed. "That means that Harm must be in the cabin. Come on. Let's go get him!"

Ed was ready to start a raid on the cabin when Don pulled him back.

"Let's sit down and think this thing over," he said. "If we rush the cabin we'll probably find Harm but it's a cinch that Uncle Bob and George Huckins are not in there. They're hidden in some more inaccessible place and if we sit tight and wait they'll lead us to this hiding place. Then we'll be able to rescue all three of them."

Ed agreed that Don's reasoning was sound and they sat down to await developments. It was a tedious vigil for no one went in or out of the cabin and the afternoon sun moved slowly on its westward course.

"I'm getting hungry," said Ed. "Let's have a whack at the lunch we had put up at Walford."

They opened the cardboard box in which their lunch had been packed. There were sandwiches and apples and the sandwiches were thick and soft.

"This bread is home-baked," said Ed. "Honestly, I don't know when food has tasted better."

"I'm pretty hungry, too," confessed Don, "and this waiting for something to happen is getting on my nerves."

They finished their lunch and resumed the steady

watch on the cabin. The sun settled behind the western hills and a purple haze crept in from the lake. It was dark enough for a light in the cabin but no gleam came from any of the windows. The first sign of life was a few minutes after sunset when the door of the cabin was opened and a man stepped out and walked down the incline to the beach.

"That must be the fellow we know as the man with the scar," Don whispered. "He's the right build. Out here he's known as Barton, according to Harm's letter."

Barton shoved the rowboat into the water and placed the oars in the locks. Then he returned to the cabin. It was evident from his whole manner that he had no idea anyone might be watching.

When he reappeared several minutes later he was accompanied by another man, who walked in a stiff, painful manner. Night was settling rapidly but even at that distance Don and Ed instantly recognized Harm, and Don had a difficult time in keeping Ed from rushing out and spoiling all their plans.

Harm's arms were bound behind him and Barton helped him into the rowboat. Then he took his own place at the oars, used one of them to shove the boat off the beach, and headed the craft out into the lake.

"We'll lose them now," complained Ed.

"No we won't," promised Don. "Look!"

A flash of light appeared on one of the islands midway across the lake. It was repeated several times and the newspapermen knew that it was a signal to guide Barton.

"Harm mentioned one other man being here in his letter," said Don, "so that light means he's on the island. Come on. We'll take a look at the interior of this cabin."

They marked the island Barton was heading for and then entered the cabin. Only a faint light came through from the windows but it was sufficient for them to get a general idea of the objects in the main room and they marveled at the completeness of the furnishings.

"If Barton owns this place it means he's got plenty of money," said Ed.

Don nodded and turned his attention to two bedrooms which opened off the main room. In one of them he found what he had been looking for—a can of grease paint and a make-up kit.

"There's no question now," he told Ed. "Curt Barton and the man with the scar, or Otto Bauer, are one and the same. And unless I'm way wrong, Barton is also Curt Boldt, who escaped from the state prison thirty years ago. The chap out on the island is probably the third member of the gang, Put Breese."

"How about Sam Corvin, the ringleader?" asked Ed.

"I can't answer that question," said Don. "Maybe it will answer itself when we get those other fellows."

Ed rummaged into a desk in one corner of the main room and came upon several ledgers that he felt might be interesting.

"Do we dare risk a light in here?" he asked Don.

"It will be safe if we go in one of the bedrooms," was the reply.

They found matches on a smoking stand and carried the ledgers into the bedroom furtherest from the lake, closed the door and drew the shade at the window. In the uneven light cast by the matches, they skimmed through the books and Don looked at Ed in amazement.

"Do you realize what these mean?" he asked.

"I'm beginning to," replied Ed.

"We've stumbled on the confidential records of one of the largest bootlegging syndicates in the middle west. These books are a complete record of their activities, purchases, sales, profits and who the profits went to."

"Do you get the names?" chuckled Ed. "We're certainly on the right trail. The profits are split three ways between Curt, Put and Sam."

"Which means Curt Boldt, Put Breese and Sam Corvin, the jail breakers of thirty years ago."

"Boldt and Breese are here," pointed out Ed. "But where's Corvin?"

Don scorched his fingers on a low burning match

but when he straightened up he was smiling.

"I don't know who Corvin is masquerading as to-day," he replied, "but I'm positive that he is in Porter. We'll find some way to scare him into the open. Now let's find a way to get out to that island."

Chapter XIX

VOICES OF THE NIGHT

Don and Ed found an old boat back of the cabin. They carried it down to the beach and shoved it into the water.

"It leaks pretty badly but I guess it will stay up until I can reach that island," observed the managing editor.

"How about oars?" asked Ed.

"They seem to be a minus quantity. I'll have to use a board for a paddle. If you can find an old bucket toss it in. I may have to bail before I get there."

"Where do you get that 'I may have to bail'?" asked Ed indignantly.

"This is a solo trip," replied Don. "Those ledgers are too valuable to leave here unguarded and then if something should happen that I don't return from the island you'll be able to take the alarm back to Walford. Besides, I don't think this leaky old scow would carry both of us."

Ed urged heatedly but without avail and Don pushed out into the lake. Using an old board they had found along the shore, he paddled industriously and soon disappeared from Ed's sight.

The island which was Don's destination was not more than a quarter of a mile from shore, a distance for which he was grateful since the old craft was leaking like a sieve and he had to stop frequently and bail.

As he neared the island he made every effort to muffle the movement of his craft. There were no lights showing along the rocky shore but he intended taking no chances. He nosed the flat-bottomed craft along a ledge of rock and scrambled ashore, where he crouched and listened for some sound which would indicate that his arrival had been observed.

A gurgling sound behind him caught his attention and he whirled just in time to see the old rowboat disappear beneath the surface of the lake. He was marooned on the island!

Under any other circumstances the situation might have been alarming but there were so many more important things that Don refused to let the sinking of his boat worry him. If necessary, he could easily swim to shore.

He soon discovered that the rock formation of the island he was on was anything but common. Sharp limestone walls enclosed the entire island, making a saucer of it. The inside of the saucer was filled with scrub oak, a few pines and a tangle of underbrush that made progress difficult.

Don moved slowly along the rocky wall which bordered the lake, hunting for the boat Barton had used only a short time before. He found it in a small cove, drawn up alongside a rock ledge that made a natural landing stage.

Moving carefully, he hunted for the trail they must have taken back into the island but search as he might he could find no sign of a path leading away from the cove. Half believing that his eyes might be playing tricks on him, Don pushed his way through the underbrush toward the center of the island. The wind was rising with a peculiar moaning that sounded almost human and the rustling of the frost-nipped leaves which fell at the command of the night wind added to the uncanny atmosphere of the mysterious island.

Don reached the center of the island without finding any sign of the men he sought and he sat down under a scrub oak to try and figure it all out.

The man they knew as Barton had brought Harm, a prisoner, to the island. He had been guided to the landing by another man with a light, which meant that at least three men were on the island for Barton's boat had been moored when he arrived. Don was also convinced that his uncle and George Huckins would be found wherever Harm was held captive, which meant that they, too, must be on the island. It was unbelievable that five men could disappear on such a small area and Don resumed his search.

He made his way to the far side of the island and then circled the entire rocky shore-line without finding a single clue. It was baffling, tantalizing and he resolved that he would not leave until he had solved the island's secret.

The next possibility was a cave, and, starting from the cove where Barton's boat was moored, Don hunted painstakingly for some opening in the rocks. There were plenty of fissures in the limestone but none that he could find that were large enough for a man to slip through into any subterranean cavern.

Don was near the middle of the island again when he stopped suddenly. Someone had cried out!

He wheeled and listened intently. The cry came again. It was hardly human, an eerie, penetrating shriek that chilled him to the bone and sent creepy shivers up and down his spine.

The wind was whipping over the island now and the cry came from the opposite direction, an agonized wail of torment. The branch of a tree brushed his cheek and he jumped involuntarily.

Had Barton found out he was on the island? Were they playing a game with him and leading him into a trap? Those thoughts crowded rapidly through his mind when the cry came a third time. It was terrifying in its sheer horror and he felt his flesh turning cold.

The moaning of the wind added to the terrors of the night and a less resolute character than Don might have fled from the island. He took a firm grip on his nerves and continued his search for a possible entrance to a cave.

The uncanny cries came again and again, sometimes near and sometimes far away as though the creature from whose lips they came were moving around the island. Don attempted to trace them but failed as the wind veered from one direction to another. Then just as suddenly as the cries had burst upon his startled ears he found the source of the weird noises. They were coming from fissures in the limestone. The wind, whipping through cracks in the rocks, moaned and cried as though in mortal agony, and the saucer-like sides of the island threw the sound back with startling sharpness.

The discovery eased the tenseness of Don's nerves and he felt calmer as he continued his search around the island. At the end of another hour he had covered almost every foot of the island and failed to find anything that even resembled an entrance to a cave. It was possible that Barton had left his boat in the cove simply as a decoy and continued in another craft but Don finally rejected that idea as unlikely.

The wind whipped around in another direction and the unearthly cries which had startled Don earlier came again and with them was born the idea that was eventually to solve the mystery of the island. It was a startling theory, one so fantastic that he hardly dared believe it, yet he determined to build all of his hopes around it and he prepared to return to the mainland.

Choppy waves were beating against the rocky shores and Don faced a long, cold swim. There was nothing to be gained by waiting and he stripped off his clothes, found a short piece of log and strapped them on with his belt. Towing the log behind him, he started for shore. The water was cold and he swam vigorously. When he reached the beach in front of the cabin Ed was waiting for him.

"What news?" the reporter asked anxiously.

"I couldn't find them," Don admitted, "but I've got a grand theory. If it works we'll have Uncle Bob, George Huckins and Harm with us tomorrow night and have the other three in custody."

"But there are only two others out there on the island," Ed reminded him.

"Yes, I know," replied Don, "but I'm going to try and drive Sam Corvin into the net, too. He's the most important one of the whole lot. Think what this will mean if we succeed, Ed. We'll have the gang that broke jail so many years ago, crush the biggest liquor ring in this part of the middle west and have Uncle Bob back in time to save the *Press* from falling into the hands of Marcus Krieg."

"It sounds great," enthused Ed. "How are you going to do it?"

"The first step is for you to stay on guard here," replied Don, "and see that they don't leave the vicinity of Lake Okoboji. I'll start back to Porter at once and will return tomorrow afternoon or early in the evening in time for the showdown. And, if anyone arrives in a hurry late tomorrow afternoon, keep out of sight."

"I'll do it," promised Ed, "but don't forget to bring a lunch along when you come back. I'll be just about starved by that time."

Don promised not to forget the lunch and set off on foot for the car on what was to prove the last and biggest adventure.

Chapter XX

EXTRA!

Don reached the *Press* office in Porter shortly after seven o'clock the next morning and found Steve on the job and planning for the day's editions. Before the city editor could ply him with questions, he outlined briefly what had happened and sketched his plans.

"I want an extra on the street at noon," he said, "with enough newsboys to carry it to every street and alley of this town. The story I'm going to write will be a sensation and it must be put into the hands of the man who thirty years ago was known as Sam Corvin. I've learned that he's somewhere in Porter, hidden now under another identity, and he must be scared into leading us to the place where Uncle Bob, George Huckins and Harm are hidden."

Don was weak from the strain of the long drive and lack of food and he took time enough to go to a nearby restaurant and have a hearty and nourishing breakfast. When he returned to the office, the business manager was waiting for him.

"I hear the showdown is near," said Hendricks.

"I'm staking everything on this one hope," admitted Don.

"Let me know if there is anything I can do," replied

Hendricks, "and I've promised Steve that there'll be a hundred newsboys to handle the noon extra."

"Thanks," said Don. "I'll probably call on you this afternoon for we'll be going back to the hills in a hurry."

The managing editor sat down at his desk to write the story for the extra. He worked steadily for an hour and when he had finished he had a story that would startle the entire town.

In bold and determined strokes he painted the entire picture of the abduction of his uncle and his friend, George Huckins, of the murder of the air mail pilot and of the kidnapping of the star reporter. Don linked it all together, going clear back to the prison escape of years before and bringing it up to the present activities of the gang, the bootleg liquor business.

In conclusion, Don wrote:

"Sam Corvin, leader of this unscrupulous band, is masquerading somewhere in Porter under another identity. Perhaps he is among us as one of our first citizens, a modern Dr. Jekyll and Mr. Hyde. But no matter who he is or how careful his disguise, the trail of circumstances is about to trip him up and the *Press* promises its readers that it will have conclusive information tomorrow."

Don turned the story over to Steve to copyread and headline.

"This is a great yarn," exclaimed the city editor, "but haven't you any idea who Corvin may be?"

"Not the slightest," replied Don. "That's why I'm taking such a chance in promising that we will have more to tell our readers tomorrow. It means that we must rescue Uncle Bob and the others tonight."

When the proofs on the story came in from the composing room, Don read them himself and then went out to check over the headlines and the front page makeup. They were satisfactory and he went down to see the business manager.

"It may be desperate business tonight," he calmly told Hendricks, "and I want to go back prepared for any emergency."

"Then I'm just the man you want," said the business manager. "I was a crack machine gunner in the war and I know where I can get hold of one of those submachine guns right now. I'll also get some guns for the rest of the boys. Who's going to make the trip?"

"Steve and you and I," replied Don. "Ed is standing watch at the lake."

"Hadn't we better take an officer with us?" asked Hendricks.

"I'd like to," replied Don, "but I'm afraid any of the local police will send the word along to the mayor, which might not help our cause."

"I can arrange that, too," smiled Hendricks. "I've a

friend who is in charge of the special police of the Great Western railroad. He's deputized and has authority to act anywhere within the boundaries of the state. What time do you want to start?"

"It's a long, slow drive," replied Don. "The noon extra should be pretty well all over town by one o'clock and if it works we'll want to be on our way by that time. Suppose we try and get away from the office at twelve-thirty or a little later."

The business manager agreed and it was decided that they would start for the Indian hills just after the extra came out.

The extra went to press on time with eight column headlines blazoning Don's story to the readers; and the newsboys, especially instructed to yell their loudest, swarmed through the streets with bundles of papers.

The members of the expedition met in the garage at the rear of the building. Hendricks arrived, carrying a sturdy cardboard carton in his arms and behind him came a stocky little man with bristly, sandy hair whom the business manager introduced as Flint Rogers, head of the special agents for the Great Western.

Don also had a bulky bundle, which, he explained, contained two collapsible canvas boats.

"We'll need them to get over to the island," he added.

A fast, powerful touring car had been made ready for them and Steve took the wheel.

"I'm fresher than you," he told Don. "You'll need all of your energy later."

It was dusk when they reached Walford and Don stopped long enough to ask the night watchman if anyone had gone out the lake road. He was relieved to get a negative answer and they resumed their journey. When they came to the fork in the road, Don had Steve wheel their touring car behind underbrush that would conceal it and they turned off the lights and sat down to await developments.

Half an hour passed and the night thickened. An hour elapsed and the moon struggled through the clouds. They moved restlessly, tense and nervous from the vigil.

They welcomed a break in the monotony when the lights of an automobile flashed down the road, the sound of a laboring motor came to their ears.

A minute later a large sedan skidded up to the forks, made the sharp turn and took the trail to Lake Okoboji.

"There goes our man!" cried Don. "After him!"

Steve started the motor of their own car and whirled it onto the trail. He reached to turn on the lights when Don knocked his hand away from the switch.

"We'll drive without lights," he said. "Do the best you can."

The tail light of the machine they were following disappeared and they bounced and skidded along the rough trail. When they were a mile from the lake Don called a halt.

"Leave the car here," he said. "If we go any closer the sound of the motor will give us away."

They unloaded the two collapsible boats and Hendricks handed Don and Steve compact little automatics.

"I hope we won't have to use them," said the business manager, "but we'll be prepared for any emergency."

Hendricks himself carried the stubby little machine gun which he had assembled on the trip down from Porter.

Don and Steve picked up the boats and they started the last lap of the journey to the lake on foot.

When they reached the clearing they found Ed anxiously awaiting their arrival.

"About time you got here," exclaimed the reporter. "Someone drove in about twenty minutes ago. He signalled the island and the boat came and got him."

"What happened today?" Don wanted to know.

"Nothing .unusual," replied Ed, "except that I'm about starved to death."

"Just before dawn Barton returned from the island and just after sundown he went back. Looked like he took some food supplies with him."

"We'll know in a few minutes," said Don grimly as he started to unfold the collapsible boat. Five minutes after they were ready to start for the island.

Steve and Ed quarreled over who should be the fourth member of the party since the boats would carry only two apiece and it was finally decided that Ed, who had waited so patiently at the lake, should have a hand in the climax. Steve regretfully turned over his gun and helped them shove the boats off shore.

The canvas crafts at best were tipsy affairs and their haste did not add to the safety but they finally negotiated the quarter mile to the island without mishap.

They landed several hundred feet below the cove where Barton kept his rowboat and Don gave them all explicit instructions before they got out of the boats.

"The mystery of the island centers around the cove," he explained, "and if our quarry has been scared as I hope by the story in today's *Press,* they'll leave the island tonight. Don't shoot unless you're forced to."

They all agreed that they understood the part each was to play and proceeded cautiously along the rocky edge of the island. The night wind was whispering softly in the stub oak and moaning through the cracks in the limestone.

The sky had cleared and the late September moon looked down on them with a chilly eye. They circled the cove, careful to keep in the shadows. When they were in their positions, they sat down to await developments.

Barton's boat was in plain sight and they knew that

the men they sought had only one means of escape
from the island. Don half expected the rocks he was
setting on to open and disclose the entrance to a cave
for he had decided that the hiding place must be some
kind of a subterranean chamber with a cleverly concealed entrance.

They shifted uneasily as the wind continued its
mournful wail and their muscles stiffened in the raw
night air.

Suddenly Ed who was crouched beside Don grasped
the managing editor's arm. His teeth chattered and
Don wondered whether it was from cold or terror.

"Look!" gasped Ed pointing toward the lake.

Don looked in the direction Ed indicated and his
blood froze in his veins. No wonder Ed's teeth had
chattered.

The moonlight played on the waves the wind rippled
along the surface of the water in the cove and in the
center a great, round yellow eye stared up at the
heavens.

Then it started moving toward shore, slowly relentlessly. Don blinked hard to make sure that he was not
seeing things but the great yellow eye came on, moving
closer to the shore, and almost unbelievable, another
and another appeared in the water until six of the weird
things were moving in upon them. Three were in a
row with two in front and one behind.

"What are they?" demanded Ed.

"I don't know," replied Don. "Wait!"

A gasp from the other side of the cove told him that the business manager and the special officer had caught sight of the great yellow eyes which were advancing toward them.

The scene changed rapidly and the bright moonlight helped them in solving the mystery. The great eyes were the glass observation sections of underwater helmets which fitted snuggly over the head and shoulders of the wearers and as they watched, six men emerged from the waters of the lake. They walked slowly toward the ledge where Barton's boat was moored and as they came, they removed their helmets. Even before the glass and metal devices had been removed from the three close together Don recognized his uncle and Harm. The third man must be George Huckins.

The other two in the lead were Barton and the man Harm had seen at the cabin on his first visit but the sixth man, the one to the rear, remained the mystery. He was large and heavy and he made slow progress toward shore, tugging at his helmet as he came.

The climax of the drama was at hand and Don and his allies leaped out from their hiding places.

"Don't move!" cried Don as the moonlight glinted off the gun he held in his hand.

Barton and the man with him obeyed the command but the man to the rear still struggled with his helmet. It finally gave way and splashed into the water and Don stared into the face of the man he believed to be Sam Corvin, prison breaker and bootleg liquor king, the man who was responsible for the abduction of his uncle, of George Huckins and of Harm; the man who had laid the plot which had resulted in the death of the air mail pilot. He might be Sam Corvin to some but to most of those present he was known as Marcus Krieg, the crooked mayor of Porter.

The shock of the sudden denouement left Don helpless and he stared at Krieg. The man in the water blinked hard at them as his eyes accustomed themselves to the light. Perhaps he saw only Don and Ed for he reached for a gun and levelled the weapon at them. There was a flash and the crack of a shot. Lead sung past Don's head and spattered against the rocks behind him.

Before Krieg could fire again there was a stab of flame from the other side of the cove. The gun dropped from his hand and without a word he disappeared beneath the surface.

Chapter XXI

A NEW DAY DAWNS

The September dawn was tinging the eastern sky with scarlet when they gathered in the editorial office of the *Press* to compare notes and discuss the sudden and startling conclusion to the mystery which had baffled them.

Sam Corvin, known to them as Mayor Krieg, was dead, the victim of the bullet from the gun of the special officer. Curt Boldt, also known as Otto Bauer and Curt Barton, and Put Breese were in jail awaiting the filing of murder charges in connection with the death of the pilot of the air express.

Robert Durian, publisher of the *Press,* George Huckins, former warden at the state prison, and Harm Nichols, the star reporter, had been freed and all danger that the *Press* might fall into the hands of the unscrupulous mayor had vanished. Instead, it was to be only a matter of days until the *Press* would take over its afternoon rival, the *Midwest News.*

Gathered in the news room, they discussed every aspect of the mystery.

"What I'd like to know," said Don, turning to his uncle, "is how you linked the escaped convicts of thirty years ago with the Mayor?"

"As a matter of fact, I didn't," replied the publisher. "That was pure coincidence. As you know I had long suspected Krieg of being a crook and our continued editorial attacks against him were based on this belief. The real credit goes to Huckins, who has been on their trail for years. Their escape almost wrecked the honor system he was installing in the prison but he managed to survive the criticism and a number of men who benefited by that system were grateful to him. Through them he managed to eventually get track of Corvin and his associates.

"Corvin came to Porter, where he became a power in local politics. When prohibition came he saw an opportunity to make illegal profits in liquor and he sent for Boldt and Breese, who had been living in Mexico. Krieg had the brains to make the plans and Boldt had the nerve. Breese was just a necessary evil, the weak one of the three.

"It was natural for them to keep tab of Huckins for they knew he would not rest until he caught them, and when they learned that we were conferring in Beldon, they quite naturally decided that Huckins had traced them and was giving me information for an exposure. Boldt was the man who boarded the plane at Beldon and when we got over the Indian hills he forced me to get into a parachute and jump. Before he made the leap he shot the pilot.

"Breese was waiting for us in a car and took us to the lake, where they made their headquarters. In the meantime Mayor Krieg got hold of that note against the *Press* and saw an opportunity to muzzle his worst enemy. But what I'd like to know is how you guessed about the cave."

"There simply wasn't any other explanation," replied Don. "I knew that Harm was somewhere on the island and a cave was the only possible hiding place. How they got into it puzzled me for I couldn't find an entrance."

"It was quite a trick," said Harm, "but those underwater helmets were the real thing. They kept several hidden on the island and the others down in the cave. With one of those on you could walk on the bottom of the lake without trouble. The cave was pretty cold and uncomfortable and the wind whistled down the fissures with a cry like someone in mortal agony."

"Don't I know it," chuckled Don. "It scared me half to death last night."

"The grease paint scar Boldt used was what bothered me," said Harm, "but when I found him at the cabin here I was sure he was the man I had trailed up from Porter even though the scar was missing. He read my message to you at the station in Walford and then hurried in to Porter and kidnapped me when I reached the *Press* building."

"We heard a shot," said Steve. "Did he try to shoot you?"

"No," replied Harm. "The shot was accidental. He clubbed me with the butt end of his gun and it went off. It's a wonder the bullet didn't hit him."

"Boldt was the key man," said Don. "He kidnapped Uncle Bob and then when he learned we had found the suitcases in the plane he was afraid we might find something incriminating and he hurried on here. He's the one who cracked you over the head when you found him trying to get into the baggage compartment of the car," he told the business manager.

"He did a good job," replied Hendricks, whose head was still sore.

"Ed's trip to Beldon precipitated the kidnapping of Huckins," Don went on to explain, "and about that time every clue we were working on faded. It wasn't until Boldt tried to rifle Uncle Bob's office and Harm trailed him into the hills that we really got down to business and then things moved fast after that."

"I'll say they did," put in Ed. "They moved so fast I've missed most of my meals for the last two days and I doubt if I'll ever be the same. I understand we'll get the reward the air express offered and I'm going to use my share buying food."

"You boys have done a fine piece of work," said the publisher, "and I'm mighty proud of you. A group of dangerous criminals has been rounded up, the *Press* is safe and the city of Porter has certainly benefited by the removal of its corrupt mayor even though that removal was a little sudden. Arrangements will be made within the next few days for us to take over the *Midwest News* and I want you to know that you'll have your same positions on the combined papers at salary increases that should be pleasing. Now let's go out and have breakfast."

"And after that," added Don, "we'll start work on the first edition."

THE END

.

www.ingramcontent.com/pod-product-compliance
Lightning Source LLC
Chambersburg PA
CBHW030257200626
46816CB00002BA/674